Partners in Crime

It seemed simple at first—two teenagers missing. But underneath was something more tangled, sinister; and in the end it turned into a nightmare. And it was my first case.

My name's Winterbottom—James Winterbottom—and when two of my schoolfriends go missing I decide to solve the mystery using the methods of that great fictional detective, Sherlock Holmes. I need someone to act as my Dr Watson, but at Haggerton High the choice is between the bully Dean, the loyal but dim Brian, and computer freak Adam. The idea of a female assistant has never entered my head.

My name's Prescot—Emmeline Prescot—and I determine to solve the mystery using the technique of that great female sleuth Miss Marple. I need someone to act as my assistant, but having dismissed the boy-mad Natalie, the superior Yasmin, and the street-wise Amelia, there is only one possibility left—James Winterbottom.

So the two sleuths become reluctant partners. But can the combined talents of Sherlock Holmes and Miss Marple succeed when the local police are baffled? And will anyone take them seriously when they unearth the clues that will solve the missing teenagers mystery?

Robert Leeson was born in Cheshire in 1928 and has been writing stories since he was nine. After National Service he became a journalist, working all round Europe, the Middle East, and Scandinavia. When his children were young he started to write children's stories and had over seventy books published, including five novels linked to the *Grange Hill* and *Tucker's Luck* television series. He has won the Eleanor Farjeon Award and has been nominated for the Guardian Children's Award and the German Youth Award. He now lives in Hertfordshire and when not writing enjoys gardening, walking, and listening to music. *Partners in Crime* is his first novel for Oxford University Press.

OTHER OXFORD FICTION

Between You and Me
Julia Clarke

Summertime Blues
Julia Clarke

Stop the Train
Geraldine McCaughrean

Getting Rid of Karenna
Helena Pielichaty

Never Ever
Helena Pielichaty

Shopaholic
Judy Waite

Partners in Crime

Robert Leeson

OXFORD
UNIVERSITY PRESS

For Christine—with thanks

OXFORD

UNIVERSITY PRESS

Great Clarendon Street, Oxford OX2 6DP

Oxford University Press is a department of the University of Oxford.
It furthers the University's objective of excellence in research, scholarship,
and education by publishing worldwide in

Oxford New York

Auckland Bangkok Buenos Aires
Cape Town Chennai Dar es Salaam Delhi Hong Kong Istanbul
Karachi Kolkata Kuala Lumpur Madrid Melbourne Mexico City Mumbai
Nairobi São Paulo Shanghai Taipei Tokyo Toronto

Oxford is a registered trade mark of Oxford University Press
in the UK and in certain other countries

British Library Cataloguing in Publication Data available

ISBN 0 19 275212 X

1 3 5 7 9 10 8 6 4 2

Typeset by AFS Image Setters Ltd, Glasgow

Printed in Great Britain by
Cox & Wyman Ltd, Reading, Berkshire

1 *James*

It seemed simple at first—two teenagers missing. But underneath was something more tangled, sinister; and in the end it turned into a nightmare.

And it was my first case. I had to have a partner. But just why, me being me, I chose a six-foot,[1] red-haired, hockey-playing feminist, needs to be explained. And it will be.

But enough about Emmeline Prescot for the moment. To get back to myself. I'll get the hard bit over first. My name's Winterbottom—James Winterbottom. James I quite like. Winterbottom I put up with; it was Dad's name, after all, all I have left of him. As you can guess, the name inspired incredible feats of wit: in Junior School it was Snowbum; in the comp, Frozen-arse. I blame the education system.

---

[1] 1.7 metres, or 5'10", actually. Typical male response to an independent female is to exaggerate. Things like 'you scare me to death', for example.—E. P.

I viewed it all with disdain. It was good training for life as an individualist. And that determined my choice of model when at an early age I decided to become a detective.

But first I must tell you that it was my mother who put the idea into my head. She was an expert in such matters as the integrity of the scene, fingerprints on the chocolate biscuits, a suspiciously smooth surface to the sugar bowl, minute traces of mud on the lino. No matter how skilled I became in covering my tracks, she would detect the crime—and took great satisfaction in telling me the clues that led to my conviction.

That was while Dad was alive. After he died, she stopped bothering, though she didn't stop caring. He was drowned at sea, the first mystery I ever tried to solve—not a case, because no crime was involved, just a strange accident.

Anyway, over the years I fantasized about becoming a detective—not a real life detective since they don't go in for detection but just act on information received—or slip wads of notes to grasses.

My chosen model was Sherlock Holmes. I'm basically a loner. He had 'a disinclination to form new friendships' ('The Greek Interpreter'). Physically we are alike—both pale (though I'm not tall). I never exert myself. He 'looked on aimless bodily exertions as a waste of time' ('The Yellow Face'). My only sport is swimming long distance non-competitive.

Like him I have a 'cold, precise, and balanced mind' ('A Scandal in Bohemia'). I go in, not for lateral thinking, but circumferential thinking—going all round a problem. I find that being too direct just gets you thumped.

I'm unashamedly elitist but have never sought to be

top of the class, a position I could achieve with ease. But I despise the pathetic efforts of top pupils to maintain their superiority.

Unlike Holmes I do not play the violin and don't do cocaine. I don't even like Coca-Cola.

Like Holmes I have 'an aversion to women' (Mum doesn't count in this case). Their illogical emotionality interferes with one's intellectual precision. I am aware of their particular nature having read *Men are from Mars, Women are from Venus*, which I borrowed from the library believing it to be science fiction.

So a female assistant in the cold detached business of detection would never have occurred to me. Indeed Emmeline Prescot might never have impinged on my mind had I not seen her one day thundering down the pitch like a tank on fire, hockey stick aloft, with Ms Frazer shrieking, 'Emmeline! Not above the shoulder!' which I took to mean head injuries were ruled out but anything below was OK.

Let me make one thing clear at the outset. I saw her in passing. I was not—repeat not—one of those pathetic voyeurs who throng the touchlines drooling over flashing thighs and dark materials (and I don't mean Philip Pullman's novels either).

So Emmeline Prescot came into my life as a partner in the business of detection. And it must be said it was the case itself which decided who I had to work with.

2 Emmeline

I first noticed Winterbottom out of the corner of my eye as I headed for goal at a rate of knots. He stood slightly apart from that small crowd of what Amelia Hardy charmingly describes as 'touchline toe-rags', and I remember him only because his face resembled Harry Potter on a bad day.

Do not suppose from this that I am vain about my own appearance. I am rather tall and my hair is an unusual sort of red—more a marmalade colour, and the rough-cut rather than the exclusive Oxford sort. The combination of height and hair sometimes leads father, when I'm depressed for some reason, to say I look like an orang-utan in the wet monsoon. Twenty years in the Overseas Mission has not improved him.

These things are, in any case, beneath contempt to a feminist, and so I regard them.

One might not have thought feminism and an enthusiasm for hockey went together, but if so, one would not have known Great-grandmother, my role model.

At the age of 15, she, who had been called Grace, re-christened herself Emmeline after the great suffragette Pankhurst. And at the age of 26 she captained a celebrated women's roller-skating hockey team. If you think this is fantasy, the files of the *Illustrated London News* hold a picture of them in action, an awesome sight in long skirts and rippling bloomers. And when you think of it—a perfect example of emancipation.

Well, in the end, the great Emmeline Pankhurst turned Tory, for which Great-gran forgave her. I overlook it, since feminists must come in all shapes, colours, and sizes. Some, like myself, believe in the natural superiority of women over men.

Some future time may see men dispensed with altogether and the species reproduced by parthenogenesis[2] (and those who don't understand that word shouldn't be reading this).

Great-gran did the next best thing. At 39, after a wild affair with a peer of the realm, she brought up her baby daughter on her own, refusing to reveal the father's name.

Her daughter (my gran) grew up quite contrary to her—married a life peer, became respectable, and sent her daughter (my mother) to a very exclusive girls' school. Not content with that she left money to send the next generation (me) to the same ghastly place. I went to the Prep School for four years and the less said of that the better. Rebelling, I demanded, at 11, to go to the local comp—in defiance of Gran's legacy.

---

[2] Typical arrogance. It means reproduction without fertilization, or do-it-yourself, like greenfly.—J. W.

Mother had hysterics, but father said, 'Let her go—the money can go to your ma's second choice—the cats' home.'

When I discovered Haggerton High played hockey, though not on skates, I was fulfilled, or almost. But, at the age of 14, I revealed a hidden talent for detection. Rummaging through the books in my parents' combined libraries, I discovered Great-gran's long-lost diary.

This told me all about her. It transformed my life. I immediately changed my own name to Emmeline. I became a feminist—and, more gradually, developed the ambition to be a detective. Not a professional one, since real-life female detectives seem to spend their lives fighting off gropers in the station canteen. But an amateur or fictional detective.

There lay another problem. Most fictional women detectives are either intellectually conceited or obsessed with sex—the opposite sex. Where could I find a model? By a process of elimination I found myself left with Miss Marple.

She has faults—she witters and she's rather snooty about charladies and gardeners. My mother witters, too, but she's afraid of charladies and gardeners. Miss Marple's appeal to me is the way she hides her shrewdness behind a vague smile, or simper. I don't simper all that well but I have no problems in disbelieving things said to me.

Miss Marple, too, manages without a partner or assistant, but she is very adept at finding someone to help her when she needs help. So, too, when I approached my first case I realized I must find someone to help me. And in the end, as you will see, that someone proved to be Winterbottom.

I was not entirely accurate in saying he was like Harry Potter because he does have a very sharp nose—a promising nose. Not, I hasten to add, that his physical appearance affected me one iota. I was interested in the mind behind the nose and how it might be used.

Things didn't turn out quite as I expected them to, however.

3 *James*

First I had to decide what sort of helper I wanted, a leg man, sidekick, or—let's be frank—a dogsbody; a henchman or lieutenant; or a full-blown partner. I was too civilized for the kind of bullying and patronizing that people like Morse, Wexford, or Dalziel go in for.

My ideal partner would be physically strong, totally loyal, bright enough to have proper conversations with but not likely to argue or contradict—someone like Watson in fact.

Looking around my year—you can get to know people pretty well when you're locked up with them most of the day, every day, every week most of the year—I narrowed the choice down to three. Dean Scully (Dean Scully was strong all right—and tough, trainee black belt), Brian Thompson was loyal, Adam Crowther was intelligent.

If I could have combined them, all would have been well—but I couldn't. So I looked at them separately. And I started to run into snags.

Dean Scully, I discovered, was bad news. He'd been thrown out of the black belt class because he had 'the wrong attitude'. I knew what they meant. He'd be more likely to break my arm than do what he was told. So Scully was crossed off the list.

Brian Thompson would do anything you asked him to—he was loyal all right. The trouble was you couldn't get rid of him—he'd follow you around like a dog. And yes, you guessed—he was a bit dim.

That left Adam Crowther. He's very bright and, as I learnt, something of a computer freak. I view all the hype about the latest info-technology with contempt, of course. Computers are all right for tracing the suspect by the last two digits of their car number, but otherwise, intellectually, so much junk.

But I chatted Adam up, pretended I was eager to learn about cyberspace and soon enough was invited home where after a brief greeting to his mother who clearly worshipped him, I was taken to his room—so loaded with the latest gear there was hardly room for a bed or chair. Did he sleep? I doubt it. His nights must be spent surfing or whatever.

My trained eye immediately caught, not the hardware, but something sitting on top of his computer. It was a plastic thing, vaguely familiar, with a long tail and claws and an idiotic expression on its green face.

He read my thoughts. 'That's my monster mascot.' I said nothing, diplomatically (it takes all sorts), but my eyebrows must have twitched.

He read my thoughts again. 'Found it in a box at a car-boot sale. Fancied it—no one else could possibly have one.' Adam was an individualist and I was beginning to feel uncomfortable.

I tried to throw him off balance. Picking the green thing up I eyed him shrewdly. 'It's been bitten to death,' I remarked and cast an analytical eye over his teeth. He seemed embarrassed.

'Yeah, that's me. I chew it when I'm working problems out.'

I nodded and filed that away. Taking the opportunity I put my idea to him—how his computer expertise would be invaluable as an aid to my investigative insights. But suddenly he became alarmed. 'Oh, I'm not having anything to do with the police—the state apparatus.'

'Not to worry,' I said. 'We solve the mysteries—they take the credit—we'll be independent.'

He shook his head . . . 'I don't know.' He began to fiddle with his mouse.

I realized it was time to ease up. I put my hand on his shoulder. 'We can chat about it another time.'

His eyes were glued to the glowing screen already.

'Uhmm,' he said.

And those were the last words I got out of him—until . . . well, after a lot of other things happened.

4 Emmeline

Women detectives, it seems, don't go in for permanent sidekicks. Miss Marple recruits them when needed, just by fluttering or being charming. Now, as mentioned, I do not flutter and I'm not charming. I do not simper easily, indeed on friends' assurance I have a laugh which is almost obscene. I suppose I could put on a simper if pushed—which might deceive the short-sighted.

So I would need to be open and straightforward about recruiting an assistant—someone I could bear to be with, talk things over with, get intelligent answers from.

I am, I must admit, a natural leader. The only snag with that is that you get natural followers—loyal but dim. Like Natalie Sutton who would follow me to the ends of the earth, provided a member of the opposite sex did not appear in the corner of her eye. No, I had to say it: Natalie, being boy-mad, would not do. Since most crime of any sort is committed by males, she'd be hopeless. So I crossed Natalie off the mental list right away.

Yasmin Ali was next and I fear she had to go the same way as Natalie—but for different reasons. She is refreshingly immune to the male sex, though devastatingly attractive with gorgeous long eyelashes. She's superior material is Yasmin—too superior. Usually has her head in a book, never listens to anybody.

I made the mistake of telling her what I had in mind. She looked at me vaguely over the top of her much-thumbed *Subtle Knife* and shook her handsome head saying: 'No thanks, but come and ask me questions if you get into difficulties.'

For a second I almost flounced off, then recalled myself and strode away.

That left me with Amelia Hardy. How she came to be called Amelia I do not know—at least I didn't until later I met her mother. Amelia, or Hardy as she is usually known, which suits her, is a bad lot. She is bare-faced, cunning, extremely street-wise, often in trouble. Not the sort you take home for tea. But I thought her qualities might be put to better use and so raised the matter with her, man to man, as it were.

She looked at me through near-closed eyes, then laughed. Now *she* has a really dirty laugh. 'If it had been anyone else but you, Presie, I'd have given you one in the chops.'

I bridled (a bit like Miss Marple) then she suddenly grinned and said, 'Tell you what, you get me into the team and you're on—for a giggle.'

With that she left me brooding. She knew and I knew that Ma Frazer would probably have pups at the thought of Hardy in the hockey team. But I felt I could work on

Ma Frazer and maybe negotiate with Hardy about things like eye-gouging, foul language, and smoking in the changing rooms.

Things turned out rather differently. Hardy did not become my partner but she did provide me with my first case.

5 James

It so happened that not long into the autumn term we had a year assembly. Ms Courtney, Year Head, led this tall, thin, dark bloke on to the platform and introduced him as Detective Inspector Sharp, which seemed like an alias to me. 'I'm sure that we've all wanted, at some time in our lives, to be a detective,' she trilled.

That raised a sort of snigger. Most of them had never wanted to be anything in their tiny lives and the only ambition some of them had was to keep out of the way of detectives. I noticed that Hardy had a cynical smirk on her face. And Adam Crowther just raised his eyebrows which I found rather discouraging.

But Courtney seemed not to notice any of this. My trained eye picked out the way her attention seemed to be fixed on DI Sharp with an expression on her face over and above the call of duty.

DI Sharp gave her a quick glance back, then got to his feet and looked the audience over. I noticed Dean Scully's head go down, and one or two in the back row seemed to shrink just a little.

'Nice to meet you all,' he said then paused. 'I hope we don't get to know one another better in the future'— we all gave a dutiful titter—'unless, of course, you have ambitions to join the force.' That put a stop to all the merriment.

He then launched into statistics on how crime was on the way down, but violent crime was on the way up. What counted, said he, was public awareness—keeping the police informed of suspicious activity, keeping your gear locked up and so on.

Then he switched to new forms of crime, hi-tech criminals, frauds carried out at the speed of light by computers, hackers who broke into bank accounts and security systems. There were 3,000 cyber-attacks world-wide every year. 'PC Plod is on his way out,' he said. 'Today we need highly educated, highly trained recruits— brain as much as brawn. So when you make your career choices, give the force a thought.'

Ms Courtney was on her feet again giving DI Sharp yet another admiring glance and inviting us to speak. Hardly surprising—only two people spoke, apart from me, of course.

Adam Crowther made Sharp's eyebrows go up by saying that hacking was no crime—it was the citizen's answer to a technological dictatorship. 'Take the hacker that got into the Haggerton supermarket system and tried to change all their prices downwards. He was a public benefactor not a crook.'

'You might think so,' said Sharp from the platform, 'but I'd like to lay my hands on him. Next time he may be up to no good. The law's the law.'

Then, to my amazement, Prescot was on her feet. Until this moment I knew her only as a pair of flashing thighs and a murderous hockey stick. I was about to see her in a new light when I heard her say: 'Of course the violence is mostly male violence, isn't it? The real problem with the police force is not who is in it, but who isn't. More women police officers, more women detectives, more people who can use both sides of their brains, is what we need.'

I shot to my feet, but I was too smart to answer directly either Prescot or Adam Crowther. The detective, said I, must be detached, cold, and logical, intent upon solving the problem rather than arresting someone and putting the blame on them. What was needed was the appreciation of the kind of mental brilliance which only the amateur, the Sherlock Holmes, could apply, not some kind of crusading reformer.

It was, though I say it myself, rather a neat little speech, and I was somewhat surprised when DI Sharp thanked Prescot and Adam for their 'interesting' remarks, then added, looking at no one in particular, 'Of course, these days, the last thing we want is Holmes or Watson tramping across the scene of the crime. The professional is king. It's a career—think about it.'

Ms Courtney shot him one last lingering glance, got us all to give him a round of applause and dismissed us. I moved over to have a word with Adam Crowther. Despite his remarks, I still felt we could do business.

But he disappeared. I decided to have a word with him the next day. But the next day something happened that turned all my plans upside down.

6 Emmeline

The mystery began next day when Adam Crowther went missing. So did Amelia Hardy. The difference between the two cases was that his parents reported it immediately. Her parents waited a day because 'she often stays over with friends'.

His parents appeared on NWTV first. They looked shattered—and baffled. 'He's never spent a night away from home,' said his mother, pale-faced and biting her lip. Mrs Hardy, a brassy type with big hulk of a husband to match, put on a real show, dabbing her eyes and coming out with things like, 'And we've just won the lottery—if only little Amelia were here to enjoy it with us.'

NWTV's 'outspoken' commentator started out to look for a scapegoat right away. He didn't actually say 'one's an accident, two looks like carelessness' but he suggested the school was to blame. Both Adam and Amelia had left home that morning and not come home at night. So the school must have mislaid them.

'No,' riposted Ms Courtney, looking, I must say, very charming when interviewed. 'Our records show they came to school in the morning and were there at lunch time. They clearly vanished on the way home.'

Now I happened to know that was not true—though one can't blame Ms Courtney. At least it wasn't true about Amelia. I had seen her at lunch time to tell her of my exploratory talks with Ms Frazer about the hockey team— my side of the bargain about sleuthing together.

Hardy had given me a rather funny little smile and said she'd see me at the gate after school. And there at 3.30, she wasn't. Not a sign of her. I waited half an hour and she definitely did not leave school. So where did she go? Where, for that matter, did Adam Crowther go?

Ah, but who else was at the gate and like me waiting for someone? None other than Winterbottom. We exchanged challenging glances (our brief exchange at the previous day's police chat had not been forgotten), but did not speak.

By the end of the week the local papers had got into the act with the question 'Have the two run away together?' His parents, interviewed, were genuinely horrified. Her mother, who seemed to do the talking, said, 'She's not one for messing about with fellas.' Which caused a little eyebrow twitching at Haggerton High.

Cue DI Sharp. He loomed over the mike on NWTV looking gaunt in his regulation dirty mac and said: 'We are not ruling out any possibility . . . but for the moment we are treating the two cases as separate. On the face of it there is no obvious connection between the two young people other than attending the same school.'

So there I was with a four-day-old mystery and no partner or assistant to help me solve it. And the provoking thing was that I already knew something which no one else did—apart from Crowther or Hardy. But what to do with my knowledge? Who to share it with?

Natalie was out of the question. It would be scattered to the four winds in an instant. I shrank from telling Yasmin. I guessed she would merely turn those large dark eyes on me over the top of her book and shrug.

Yet I sensed someone else was already deeply interested in the mystery and keen to delve into it. And that someone was Winterbottom. There was clearly an intellect of sorts behind that pointed nose and dark eyes. He was, of course, the perfect paid-up woman hater—but that, I reflected, had its advantages. At least if we worked together he would concentrate on the matter in hand and nothing else.

The question was—would he accept my leadership, or at least guidance? There was only one way to find out—if you have leadership qualities, you have to take a lead.

I ambushed him on the road outside school, away from prying eyes, and put the matter to him, man to man. He looked at me very cautiously but as far as I could see with perfect frankness and said slowly, 'Where shall we meet to talk it over?'

'Behind the bike sheds,' I answered.

'Which end—smokers' or snoggers'?'

I gave him a withering glance.

'In the middle!'

He nodded and turned to go then totally threw me by saying, 'Your hair—it's just right.' I stared at him open-mouthed. Had I misread him? What hidden depths were boiling behind that pointed nose?

He turned slightly red. 'No, I mean you could be a

member of "The Red Headed League".' He paused. 'You know, the Sherlock Holmes story.'

I didn't, but couldn't afford to let him guess that, so I replied firmly, 'Of course.' Then to emphasize who was in charge added, 'Half past twelve then. Be there.'

Too late I remembered Miss Marple my role model and gave him a well-crafted winsome smile. But he'd already turned his back and was walking away up the street.

7 *James*

'It's as simple as this. We've got this missing persons case. Are you interested in helping me solve it?'

When I said these words, I had the distinct impression that Prescot was talking at the same time. And what is more she was saying more or less the same as me. It was not a good start.

We were standing behind the bike sheds, well away from the snoggers at one end and the smokers at the other. Or rather we were leaning with our backs to the corrugated iron which was comfortably warm in the sun. In front of us was a strip of rough grass too narrow to be used for games but often very convenient for pre-arranged rucks or similar rituals. Right now it was empty all the way across to the high thorn hedge that marked the end of school territory and the start of the out-of-bounds zone.

The scene in front was ideal for quiet discussion—but the opening words left a very awkward silence. I didn't look at her—because that would have meant looking upwards. And she didn't look at me. Instead we both stared across the grass. This could have gone on forever—she was clearly indulging a fit of feminine pique. I decided to take the initiative.

'Let's start with stating what we know. Hardy and Adam have gone missing.' I paused. 'And it's pretty obvious, given what we know about them, that they didn't go off together.'

'No, it's not.'

Now I did look (up) at her.

'You what?' It wasn't a very Sherlock Holmesian remark, I admit, but she surprised me. Obviously I had to get used to her shooting off in all directions. I tried to get some sort of logic into the proceedings. But when I opened my mouth I found she was looking (down) at me and talking.

'You probably missed it when we had that Assembly about the police. You were too busy trying to impress DI Sharp.'

'I—' But she was crashing on—talking the way she goes down the hockey pitch.

'I noticed that Hardy and Adam Crowther kept looking at each other. No one else could see it because they were over in the corner. But whenever anybody else spoke they'd be going nudge, nudge—with their eyebrows.'

'You're joking.' . . . it was all I could think of to say.

She shook her head, her ginger locks whipping to and fro.

'Uhuh! No way. We don't miss things like that or mistake them.'

We? Was she talking like the queen? Surely not. I realized she was making a feminist statement. I sighed inwardly—I clearly would have to cope with a lot of this kind of thing. But I stayed calm.

'OK. So we have another theory then—they went off together.'

'Not theory—fact.'

I snapped, 'The only fact we have is they've gone missing—on the same day. No, wait a minute,' I said more calmly as I remembered something. 'We do know something else.'

'Like what?' She was looking at me, frowning for some reason as though her patience was being tested. Can't think why.

'Adam Crowther at least went missing from school that day. He never went home—unless his parents are telling porkies, which I don't believe.'

'How do you know?' Ah, she was interested now.

'Because he agreed to meet me by the gate to the main road after school. And he never turned up.'

'That's funny!'

'It's significant.'

'No, I mean it's funny because Hardy made the same arrangement with me and she didn't show up either. So if you rule out coincidence, which is ridiculous, the two of them must have stayed in school somewhere and slipped away down the road later.'

'No, they didn't.' I was suddenly so excited I grabbed her by the arm. She gave me a freezing look and I let go. Instead I pointed to the hedge.

'That's the way they went.'

'What, through the thorns?'

'No,' I said patiently. 'There are gaps very low down where you can push bushes aside and squeeze through.'

'And . . . ?'

'And if you go down Haggerton Clough, about half a mile along you come to the main road.'

Haggerton Clough, I should explain, is a sort of valley with pretensions to be a ravine, with a boggy stream at the bottom, and the sides dotted with big clumps of thorn, elder, and gorse. Once through the hedge you can make your way without being seen—a fact appreciated by the powers-that-be and by those intending to outwit them.

We were both silent for a moment. Neither of us wanted to be the first to say, 'What do we do now?'

Instead we both said masterfully, 'This needs thinking over. Let's meet here again on Monday and compare notes.'

With that we each went our own way unnoticed[3] by either smokers or snoggers.

Before Prescot and I met again the case had taken a dramatic turn. The police had given up checking with forces in other cities. They began a massive search closer to home. This was ominous and had a bad effect on the school. Ms Courtney had the bright idea of organizing carefully selected volunteers to join in combing the countryside.

Our sector was Haggerton Clough and twenty of us were picked to go out with DI Sharp and his merry men. A lot more than twenty had offered—mainly for good reasons. Some at least had other things on their minds, though. On the other side of the Clough, behind a high old

[3] Not entirely unnoticed. At the end of lunch break, Natalie Sutton in her insinuating way told me, 'I saw someone meeting someone else behind the bike sheds today. Anyone special?' I remained tight-lipped but gave her a quick simper which seemed to satisfy her.—E. P.

stone wall, topped with the usual ancestral barbed wire and broken glass, were the main grounds of Haggerton Hall.

And who had recently taken over the Hall? There hadn't been a genuine Haggerton there in yonks, but Cameron Hayter, millionaire TV film star, presenter personality, heart-throb, voted my-choice-for-a-weekend-between-the-sheets by fifty million females, had arrived.

When Ms Courtney told us the search stopped short of the Hall grounds some of the eager volunteers cooled off. So picking twenty who would actually be a help rather than a hindrance proved a simpler matter.

We gathered at the end of the Clough early on Monday morning. For a September day it was going to be hot— very hot. But for the moment it was foggy and white clouds of mist hung in the hollows and wreathed round the thorn bushes. It gave the valley a spooky feel and I suddenly had the awful thought—suppose you poked under a bush and there was Adam Crowther or Amelia Hardy lying still and staring up at you.

So vivid was the picture I turned towards Prescot, who was standing not far away, to say something. Then I changed my mind—we didn't have that kind of connection, for sharing awful thoughts. Keep it detached, I told myself.

DI Sharp assembled us and gave some tips about not falling into bogs or down old canal ventilation shafts and providing the company with an unsolicited corpse. He wound up by saying, 'Just keep your eyes open for anything, repeat anything, you think might be important. If you spot anything tell one of my officers about it. Do not touch it, do not go near it. Just note and report.'

I cleared my throat. 'The integrity of the scene,' I

remarked. DI Sharp looked surprised at this kind of clued-up comment, then said, somewhat patronizingly I thought, 'No, it's not a scene, yet, laddie [laddie!]. We haven't got a crime yet.'

One or two idiots in the crowd began to snigger. I felt I had to recover the situation. I cleared my throat again. 'Won't the search include the grounds of Haggerton Hall, Inspector?'

He gave me a thin-lipped glance and said, 'Not at the moment. It's not really a very likely place.'

A phrase of Sherlock Holmes's sprang to mind. I said: 'Surely when all other possibilities have been eliminated, then what remains . . . ?'

He didn't let me finish but made some completely stupid remark[4] which he, and some of the idiots in the crowd, actually thought was witty. I said no more, merely thinking to myself: wasting my time.

The search began. Police and Haggerton High people moved slowly down the Clough towards the high ground and the thorn hedge behind which lay the school. Above us, on the south side of the valley, ran the estate wall. On the other side was the main road. So the area was clearly marked and completely covered by our line.

We could only move slowly. The ground was uneven, with sudden dips and holes and the grass was treacherous and slippery. Every few yards you ran into a thorn bush or a clump of gorse and had to crouch down to look beneath it—half hoping to find something interesting, half fearing there might be something you didn't want to see.

---

[4] What DI Sharp actually said was, 'Well, they could have been abducted by little green men.'—E. P.

Every now and then Sharp's sergeant blew a whistle. We stood up and got back into line. Then the search began again, moving more and more slowly, because by now the sun was well up and it was swelteringly hot.

I suddenly noticed Prescot, on my right. She nodded and seemed about to speak, but I gave her to understand I thought we should concentrate on the ground we were covering. She shrugged and we moved forward.

The whistle blew again and a WPC came along the line with plastic bottles of juice. 'And don't chuck the empties,' I heard Sharp bellow. 'Keep 'em with you. The integrity of the scene, you know.'

As the idiots started to laugh again I began to feel I could really detest that bloke. A bit like Inspector Lestrade in the Sherlock Holmes stories—bumptious but dim. What would Holmes do? Treat him with silent contempt till the moment came to reveal the solution to the mystery and accept his apologies and humble thanks, no doubt.

These thoughts went through my mind as I sat on the rough grass swigging my juice. Suddenly there was Prescot looming over me. Well, she was sitting really but she does tend to loom. I decided I must be diplomatic and so engaged her in conversation. Without realizing why I found myself asking her how she came to be interested in detection.

To my utter astonishment, she began to talk very earnestly about her great-grandmother (!!) and finding this diary, working out the secret of her love life and so on. It seemed fascinating, in a bizarre sort of way, and it did sort of make sense of her generally stroppy attitude. I mean with ancestors like that . . .

To be polite I told her a bit about my mother and my father and his being lost at sea. I could hear my voice rambling on giving a picture of this monster steel tanker, ploughing through the waves, a sailor falling from the bows into the night, while 400 metres away in the brightly-lit crew's quarters his mates were watching blue movies as he was sliding into the black depths.

The whistle blew. She gave me a quick tap on the shoulder, stood up, and we began the search once more. The end of the Clough was getting close and apart from a couple of false alarms—once when someone found an old plastic bag, the other when a sleeve of a jacket was seen hanging on a bush—we were drawing a big blank.

Finally, DI Sharp called out, 'Well done, everybody. We'll call it a day now. You may think it's a complete waste of time, but most of our work is elimination. And we can rule out the Clough now. There's nothing here for us.'

But how wrong he was. Two blokes had appeared at the top of the rise. They must have come through a gate in the stone wall round the Hall grounds. One was a square-built, red-faced man wearing gaiters and a leather jacket. He was a gamekeeper from the estate and looked it. The other bloke, who was about twice as big, broad shouldered, looked like a dosser. He had a ragged overcoat which half covered a hairy grubby chest, and a filthy woolly hat on top of matted hair that hung down over his face.

They came up to DI Sharp. The gamekeeper was doing the talking and I knew right away this was important. So I moved forward smartly and wormed my way through the throng till I was standing behind DI Sharp. That way I killed two birds with one stone. DI Sharp couldn't see and tell me to get lost, and I could get a good look at the two of them. I was so close that the smell of cheap cider and meths came billowing across from the dosser—

making me want to throw up. But I stayed where I was. The gamekeeper was talking and DI Sharp was listening intently.

'This is Toby. He dosses now and then in the old barn.'

'Oh yes,' said DI Sharp. 'We haven't met before.' By which I took him to mean that Toby could consider himself filed for future reference.

'He's got something to tell you.'

Toby's voice suddenly boomed out. 'Yah! Two kids— boy and a girl. They were by the main road. They woke me up—I was having a kip in the long grass. They were talking. I couldn't hear proper but she called him Addie— I'm sure of that.'

'Go on,' said Sharp.

'This car drew up—a limo. Bloke with a posh voice said . . . ''Want a lift, you two?'' They got in and he drove off—just like that!'

'When was this?'

'Err . . . dunno.' Toby counted on his fingers—then, 'Last Tuesday.'

'How d'you know?'

'Got my giro, didn't I?'

'Did you get the car number?'

Toby's florid face screwed up with indignation. 'Think I'm some kind of a grass? What d'you take me for?'

'OK, OK,' DI Sharp cut him off. 'Thank you, Mr Venables. Thank you, Toby. Now do us a favour and don't wander off for a few days. We may need to talk to you again.'

The search was over for the day. We all trickled back to school, everyone talking at once. Suddenly it was clear to all of them. Hardy and Adam Crowther had done a bunk in a posh car heading north—Leeds, Newcastle, you name it. End of mystery.

Except for me. I was thinking hard. Standing behind DI Sharp, I had a good look at Toby. His story sounded fair enough—but there was something not right about him. It was only when I was lying in bed later that night that I realized—it was his eyes.

8 Emmeline

The mystery deepened, or the plot thickened, whichever you prefer. The police took very seriously the story told by dosser Toby, though as NWTV exclusively revealed, that gentleman mysteriously vanished two days after his revelations.

I had a modest flush of satisfaction. My theory—that Adam and Hardy had run away together—had proved right. But that was followed by a sense of disappointment. What now? If the missing two had taken the road north my (or rather our) investigation was stuck. I say our in brackets because I had seen neither hide nor hair of Winterbottom ever since he had slunk away from the Clough after his humiliation by DI Sharp.

I felt sorry for him, not because of his humiliation, which, to my unbiased mind, he had brought upon himself, but after hearing the story of his father lost at sea. I often feel like losing my father when he winds me up to distraction. But I would not wish him drowned in dark waters. Irritating as they undoubtedly are, everyone can use a father. Had Winterbottom and I been friends, rather than collaborators, I would undoubtedly have said a word or two of consolation to him. But it was not that kind of relationship.

Apart from which, I told myself, with some regret, the case was out of our hands. No more intellectual meets behind the bike sheds.

How wrong I was. Before that week was out we met again—at his command. I use the word with care. You may imagine my astonishment when one lunch hour as I made my way to practice, idly swinging my stick, W. crossed my path and, with a peremptory jerk of the head, signalled towards our meeting place.

I bridled. The great-granddaughter of Emmeline Huxtable is not to be summoned by a mere twitch of a male head. On the other hand, there was on his pale face a positively radiant look and that famous nose seemed to twitch like a bloodhound's (or perhaps a ferret's) hot on the scent. Curiosity getting hold of me, I followed with what dignity I could muster. Abandoning his usual evasive pose, he looked me straight in the eye and said, 'You think those two have gone off up north, don't you?'

Before I could confirm or deny he pressed on: 'That's what they all think—police, people in school . . . ' He paused. I waited. I wasn't going to say, 'What are you driving at, old chap?' or some other rubbish such as Watson is supposed to come out with.

His impatience got the better of his pride. He burst out, 'Well, they haven't!'

I know he wanted me to ask him how on earth he knew but wasn't going to give him that kind of opening. Instead I said, 'Well, where are they, then?' (I had decided not to do the triumphant bit and remind him it was I, not he, who had insisted they had gone *together*.)

He stared at me, then made a face. 'Dunno.'

'That's not much use, is it?'

He ignored the taunt. 'I just know that story about them hitching a lift is probably rubbish.'

'You mean a dosser's word isn't enough to be trusted—that's fair enough—but it's not conclusive, is it?'

'No, you—' He censored the description. 'I mean, this character Toby isn't a dosser.'

'Don't follow. He ponged like one.'

'He may have done. At least he smelt of meths and cider—but I was close enough and there wasn't any stink of sweat and filth—you know.'

'I don't know many dossers. Maybe he'd been given a sluice in the gamekeeper's tin bath.'

He gave me a look of scorn, but said, 'Never mind the pong. It was his eyes. They were wrong. They weren't an alky's eyes—they didn't have that shifty, crafty look.'

'How do you know that?' I was astonished, impressed, and incredulous all at once. He turned slightly pink, lowered his eyes. 'I can't tell you that, yet, but you can work on the hypothesis that Toby wasn't a dosser. He was someone pretending to be a dosser.'

'So . . .'

'So, the story about Adam and Hardy going north is more than rubbish. It could be a blind.'

'A blind? But—'

I never finished the sentence. Someone else was speaking and it wasn't Winterbottom.

'Clear off. This is our patch.'

I turned. There stood Dean Scully looking big and unpleasant as always and two of his sidekicks or hangers-on. My mind worked swiftly. What would Miss Marple do? Flash them a winsome smile? No! I drew myself up—increasing my five centimetre advantage over Scully by fifty per cent.

'What on earth are you talking about?' I said crushingly. Scully was uncrushed.

'I said get lost. This is our patch.'

'*Your* . . . patch?' He misunderstood me.

'Well, it was Hardy's, but she's gone so I'm taking over.'

'Taking over what?' It's amazing the effect a forthright question has on even the most hardened individual. They answer without thinking.

'The patch—where she passes out gear!' He paused to let this sink in, then said, 'We're taking over. So you two vanish—now—and don't let me see you here again.'

I was running out of height but drew up a further two centimetres. 'We shall meet here as and when we choose. Whatever you are up to, you do it when we are not here.'

'No, we don't. You're a couple of grasses poncing around the filth, that's what you are, so **** off.'

This had gone far enough. I shifted my stick to the bully-off position, observing with some alarm that Winter-bottom was actually moving to place himself between Scully and me—though that would still leave us eyeball to eyeball over his head.

'Read my lips: **** off.' With that Scully jabbed his finger at my chest.

Now no one, but no one, fingers Miss Marple's bosom. They don't even contemplate it.

I swung the stick in an arc usually designed to catch the ball in mid-air. Here the target was stationary—the chances of missing, nil. As luck would have it,

Winterbottom, fists clenched chivalrously, had moved into the target area. Scully took the brunt of the blow, but poor Winterbottom got the rest of it at the end of the swing and flew away in his turn.

With no time to reflect I made a powerful back stroke which caught the second sidekick or hanger-on full point in a sensitive area. The third man, telling himself no doubt that honour is an empty word, took flight.

All three were in motion. One staggering slightly concussed, one walking knuckles to the ground like a demented chimpanzee, one running upright.[5]

We were alone, I flushed, W. white as a sheet with a red weal across his forehead. All violence purged, the weaker side of nature came to the fore. Not to put too fine a point on it my mother took over.

I flung my arms around him and heard myself say: 'Shall I kiss it better?'

He was not best pleased with that.

---

[5] That was not the end of the story. Brian Thompson later told me two stories were circulating at Haggerton High. One was that Dean Scully had been injured in a full-scale confrontation with rival pushers; the other that he had been held down by vigilantes and beaten with a baseball bat. His No. 2's injury was not mentioned. At all events Scully's operation quite suddenly folded.—J. W.

9 *James*

We met again the next day, same time, same place, and had the mid-shed area to ourselves. I summed up the situation succinctly, with Prescot putting in a question or two now and then.

'Hardy and Adam have gone missing. We don't know where they are but it's probably not along the main road.'

'Where then?'

'Maybe not far away. We've got to think. If we knew who was master-minding it all we'd have a clue.'

'Does there have to be a master-mind?'

'If my theory's right and the dosser is phoney, then someone's going to a lot of trouble to put the police and everyone else off the scent.'

'Except us.'

'Except us. Now we can take it that Hardy lured Adam away.'

'Oh, blame the female as usual.'

'I thought you feminists liked girls taking the lead.'

'OK, OK.'

'If Hardy lured Adam, how did she do it?'

'She's an attractive person when she decides to be charming.'

'Nah. I don't think Adam's interested in anything but hermaphrodite computers. No, my money's on drugs.'

'You reckon Adam's a user?'

'Well, we know Hardy's a pusher.'

'We know that toe-rag Scully says she is.'

'You're starting to talk like her, Prescot.'

'I'm trying to stick to facts, Winterbottom.'

'OK, OK. I think we need to know more about them. Question is—where to start? We don't want to cause too many waves at school.'

Prescot snapped her fingers. 'Got it. We start at the source.'

'Source?'

'Yes. We go and talk to the parents!'

I stared at her. 'Are you serious? Just call at their home, eh? Say we're conducting an unofficial investigation and would just like to ask some intimate questions.'

'No, no, no, Winterbottom. We are schoolfriends—anxious, full of sympathy.'

'It might work,' I said slowly.

'Course it will,' she answered. 'Look, we'll start at the Hardys'—we'll go there this evening. Now remember—it's school clobber, and leave the talking to me.'

I mastered my irritation at this blatant attempt to take charge, because it might just work and she'd take the flak if it went wrong. I *would* keep my mouth shut. And I did, though at times, that evening, I was sorely tried.

I was amazed at first how easy it was. At the Hardys'

we were ushered into this lounge where everything was wall-to-wall carpets, settee, hi-fi, TV and video. We were sat in two armchairs of the sort that swallow you up. Prescot was OK—she projected a long way. But I hoisted myself up and sat on the edge, a move which did not pass unnoticed by the husband, as he sat with his arm around his wife on the enormous settee.

I studied him, not too obviously. He was younger than her—a good bit younger. A beer-gut and a big moonlike face just made him look older—that and his eyes which were . . . sort of watchful. I began to wonder whether he may not be boyfriend or stepfather—particularly because Ma Hardy was doing the talking.

'Well, what did you want?' she demanded when Prescot had introduced us.

'We're just schoolfriends. We wanted to let you know how worried we are about Amelia and Adam and ask if you have any news.'

'Don't you watch the telly?' Ma Hardy was abrupt to say the least.

'Of course.' Prescot has this soapy manner she can put on—which I suppose she gets from her vicar father. On top of that she had what I can only describe as a totally stupid smile on her face, which she evidently thought was reasssuring. 'But we hoped you might have learned something more . . . '

'Oh yes?' Ma Hardy's tone got more hostile by the second. 'Friends, eh—that takes a lot of believing. Our girl never mixed with snobs in her life.'

Prescot didn't bat an eyelid. 'Life's full of surprises, Mrs Hardy—Amelia and I were trying to work out how she could get into the hockey team, which she was rather keen on.'

Ma Hardy gave a sort of cackle. 'Pull the other one—she never wanted to play hockey in all her born days.'

He suddenly spoke, giving her a little squeeze as he did. 'Don't upset yourself, pet. We don't know everything about our daughter, do we?' (His voice lowered a fraction on the *our* and I knew for certain he wasn't the father.) 'Perhaps Emmeline and James [He'd remembered the names—this was no idiot] can tell us things we ought to know about Amelia.'

Prescot walked right into it. 'There's a story going round school that . . . ' she paused and I could see the two of them tensing, 'she was involved in dr—'

She didn't even get to the end of that little word before Ma Hardy gave a scream you could hear up the road.

'That's a filthy lie.' She shot up, flung her arm out. 'Get out, you little . . . '

He pulled her back, and spoke quietly to us: 'Well, perhaps you'd better leave. I'm sure you mean well but that's a bit strong.'

We got to our feet and were on our way to the door when he said, 'Could you perhaps tell us who has been putting these slanderous stories about. It's bad enough losing her, losing the family name as well is too much . . . '

There was a moment's silence. I said quietly, 'No one special—just gossip, you know.'

He nodded. 'Some people'll say anything.'

As we withdrew from the Hardys' I said firmly, 'I'll do the talking at the Crowthers', OK?'

10   *Emmeline*

I ignored the implied rebuke in W.'s remark and said nothing as we headed down the road towards the Crowthers'. It seemed to me that I had put my finger on the spot. Drugs were in the frame and Hardy's parents (or mum and boyfriend) were in it as well. Maybe Hardy (Amelia) had been sent away to avoid exposure. Adam (possible addict) was removed as potential evidence.

I mused on these things in silence as we walked along. The female mind prefers this mode, hence giving rise to the male illusion, that our intellectual leaps are all to be put down to 'intuition', whatever that is.

The Crowther house was a lot quieter in every way— in fact a little dreary, perhaps—or was I just being influenced by that showroom lounge we'd just left. Lottery money, Mrs Hardy had mentioned in her TV interview. I gave a hollow laugh to myself. I had other ideas about where their money came from.

The Crowthers were a very subdued couple. I knew

they had good reason to be but just had this feeling that they were like that all the time, dressed in dark clothes, sitting in dark brown leather armchairs not saying much, reading the *Radio Times* and going to bed early. But I felt sorry for them. They were in shock. They were totally baffled.

'He was our only son.' (The mother was doing the talking again.) 'He was so quiet, though he had a very intelligent mind. His reports were so good. He never went out. He just came home from school and spent his evenings upstairs with his computer. We bought him a lot but he spent all his own money, buying new bits and pieces.'

'Hardware and software, dear,' said Mr Crowther, but she didn't seem to hear him. She was launched on her story of little Adam and Winterbottom didn't get a word in edgeways either.

'I just can't believe he went off with that Amelia Hardy. I don't at all. Did you see that awful woman on the box? Well, I shouldn't speak ill, but I can't believe that Adam really wanted to go off like that—with *that* girl. I don't think he planned to go at all. I think he was—' she looked round at us all, '—abducted.'

I thought at first she would go on talking, but I reckoned without Winterbottom. He dropped a hand grenade into the conversation.

'Excuse me, Mrs Crowther, but can I ask you: is his mascot—his green monster—still on top of the computer upstairs?'

She looked as if she'd been hit by a sandbag. Then suddenly she was up out of her chair. We heard her feet on the stairs—running up, then down again. She burst back into the sitting room.

'It's gone!'

I looked at Winterbottom and prayed that Adam's parents didn't notice that little smile on his lips. He'd proved to his own satisfaction at least that if Adam had taken his mascot then he'd known he was going away before he left the house.

'Are you sure it's gone? Not fallen on the floor, dear?' soothed Mr Crowther.

'No, no! It's always there. I've been so upset I never noticed it wasn't.'

She gave Winterbottom a glance which I suppose in the old days would go along with a wax doll full of pins. But there was more to come. Ferret like, W. was determined not to let go.

'Did you suspect that Adam might be . . . on something?'

'On something?' said Mr and Mrs Crowther in unison. Then as the penny dropped she gave a wail of despair. 'No, he'd never do anything like that—not *our* Adam.'

Mr Crowther silently saw us into the street and hurried back inside where his wife was having hysterics.

As we headed down the road, I gave Winterbottom a searing glance as if to say, 'Well, you made a fine cock-up of that', but he gave me a glance which persuaded me to keep my thoughts to myself.

We had a lot to think about. But just how much we did not know until the next day.

11 *James*

Whence we met next day, I tried to sum up what we had discovered. But in order not to sound pompous I put it in the form of questions.

'Did you notice the difference between those two families?' I asked Prescot.

She looked at me in a gormless sort of way then said, 'No, Holmes, old chap, I'm completely baffled.'

I felt a rush of blood to the head. One thing I do not like is leg-pulling about serious matters. 'If you're going to be stupid, I'm going,' I told her.

'And if you're going to waste my time with idiotic questions, I'm going,' she threw back. Then she went on more calmly, 'Honestly, Winterbottom, there were scores of differences between the Hardys and the Crowthers—decor, accent, education, way of life—get to the point.'

'OK, OK. The thing is, the Crowthers were *upset*.'

'Well, so were Ma Hardy and her boyfriend.'

'Ah.' I raised a finger, then put it down as she glared

at me. 'The Crowthers were upset because of Adam. Ma Hardy was upset because we were prying—and he—whatsisname—wasn't upset at all.'

That silenced her for a bit but then she said, 'You're right, but what d'you make of that?'

'The Crowthers don't know where Adam is but Ma Hardy and friend know where Hardy is—'

'That means they know where Adam is, too!'

'Yeah.' I ticked off my fingers. 'Hardy lured Adam away using drugs, in fact the whole thing may be drug linked.'

'That talk about lottery money,' she said, 'is a cover for their affluence . . . '

'But if they've been pushing for some time, why do they suddenly need to explain their money away? Unless . . . unless, they've suddenly been given some more money . . . '

'This is really a kidnapping disguised as a runaway,' butted in Prescot.

'Right, like the suicide disguised as a murder in Sherlock Holmes's "Thor Bridge",' I began, then stopped as another thought occurred to me. 'And what about Toby the wino? How's he connected with Ma Hardy and friend. Why was he laying a false scent? And why did he vanish?'

Before she could say 'How do you know?' I put in another question: 'Where did Toby come from and where did he vanish?'

'The Haggerton Estate,' she answered like a shot. 'You think there's a connection?'

'I think we might try and find out . . . ' I began. Then I suddenly sensed that we were not alone. Someone was watching us. I turned. About a couple of yards away stood

Natalie Sutton, a female creep if ever there was one. Before either of us could say a word she got hers in.

'They've been looking all over for you.'

'Who has?'

'Oh, Ms Courtney . . . ' She ran on, 'I knew where you two'd be so I offered to find you.'

Prescot turned on her so that she took a step back. 'Did you tell them where we were?'

Natalie simpered[6] and said in this false voice, 'Would I grass on you like that?'

'You'd better not!' Prescot turned to me, and said quietly, 'Let's go and find out.'

Ms Courtney was waiting in her office. She told us to sit down and began pleasantly enough.

'I gather you two have begun an investigation into the disappearance of Amelia and Adam. Your concern does you credit.'

I relaxed in my chair.

'However . . . '

I sat up again.

'Concern does not excuse unacceptable conduct.'

'I don't understand . . . ' I began.

A line appeared between Ms Courtney's eyes.

'Parents have complained. You two have intruded on their privacy, made insinuations about . . . substance abuse . . . '

'Which parents . . . ?' I began again then stopped. I thought Ms Courtney was going to go nova.

'This has to stop—both of you—whatever your motives, it cannot be tolerated. Playing the amateur detective is one thing but I've heard reports of brawls behind the

---

[6] Hers was a genuine simper.—E. P.

bike sheds, which quite frankly, knowing the characters of both of you, I found incredible. I hope I have not been mistaken in you.'

I was about to put Ms Courtney straight on one or two questions of fact when Prescot got me one on the ankle—a skill learned on the hockey pitch, no doubt. I shut up—in agony.

To my astonishment she spoke. She made a totally embarrassing, even grovelling, little speech. I did not believe her capable of such abysmal cringing.

When we were outside again, I turned on her. 'It was bad enough you trying to break my ankle, but that exhibition of boot-licking was revolting. Have you undergone a character change or something?' I imitated Prescot's simpering slush, 'You won't hear any more such stories, I assure you, Ms Courtney.'

Prescot took my rebuke calmly. 'I chose my words deliberately. The reason she isn't going to hear any more stories is because we are going to be more careful about what we do and who sees us.'

'So what are we going to do?'

'What you suggested,' she answered with that superior smile of hers. 'We're going to have a look at the Haggerton Estate—discreetly.'

'When?'

'After school. You on?'

'Course I'm on.'

What else could I say, even if I thought it was mad.

12 *Emmeline*

We sat on the short grass under the long estate wall. The crumbling stones were golden in the late afternoon sun.

'It's lovely here; the Haggertons must have picked the best spot in the area after 1066,' I remarked. But Winterbottom, as usual, was not listening. He was looking back anxiously across the Clough, which was dotted with these marvellous yellow gorse flowers, towards the thorn hedge we'd ducked under and the school grounds beyond.

'Do you think anyone spotted us coming over?'

'No,' I answered reassuringly. 'I made sure little Natalie had gone home before I made my move. Shall we get started?'

But he wasn't listening. 'Look at that.' He pointed to the left of the thorn hedge to a high wall with narrow windows.

'That's the science block,' I said idly. 'What's so special about that?'

'I know it's the science block. But look there—bottom right-hand corner. There's a door. You can get out on the Clough from the labs without all the hedge-hopping.'

'Million to one it's locked,' I answered. 'The powers-that-be won't leave that bolt-hole open.'

'Suppose you're right.'

Why did the thought of my being right seem to give him grief?

'Come on,' I said. He rose with me and we began to move along the wall. 'What are we looking for?' I asked.

'The gate Toby and the gamekeeper came through for a start.'

We moved slowly along the wall, looking back towards the school every now and then. The rough stone was still warm to the touch. 'Here we are,' said Winterbottom. A narrow iron gate was set into the wall. The metal was rusted. W. pushed, it creaked but did not move.

'It's locked.'

'Elementary,' I said and pointed to the padlock, halfway down the gate.

He gave me a petulant glance then smirked. 'You'll notice that the padlock is new. Someone has recently started to use this gate.'

'Or to stop other people using it,' I countered.

'OK, OK. So it's over the wall. One at a time.'

'Why?'

'So the other can keep an eye on the school—check if we're being watched.'

He moved back along the wall, well away from the gamekeeper's gate.

'Come on,' I urged and launched myself upwards. The climb was easy enough until it came to the top. I'd almost put my hand on the barbed wire and broken glass.

'Here,' whispered W. from below and passed up an old jacket he'd been carrying with him. 'I brought this on purpose,' he told me with pride.

'Good thinking,' I allowed him, and laying the jacket over the spikes I rolled over the top of the wall and dropped down on the other side. There was a disconcerting rip. My skirt had caught on a glass shard and split to the waist. I sprawled on the grass and surveyed the damage as Winterbottom, wide-eyed, landed with a thump beside me.

'Didn't bring a safety pin with you, by any chance?' I asked him.

'Sorry.' He shook his head. Winterbottom, I sadly concluded, had a mind but no sense of humour.

We looked round. The place was a wilderness; great swathes of bracken and bushes, dark clumps of trees stretched away in front of us. Above them the towers and chimneys of Haggerton Hall showed red and brown.

'It's enormous,' I muttered.

'Yeah. Let's do a recce now and then come back at the weekend to do a proper search.'

That made sense. We began to walk in the general direction of the Hall. But the bracken was waist high, the ground dipped, and bushes got in the way. Soon I was aware we'd lost sight of the Hall beyond the tree-line.

'This won't do,' muttered W. 'We're getting nowhere fast and can't see anything.'

'Look.' I pointed to the left. 'We need a vantage point. So how's about we climb up there?'

'There' was a strange lump in the landscape, like a giant square mole hill—if you can imagine such a thing. We turned towards it and it soon showed itself to be an old stone structure of sorts, maybe seven metres long, three metres high, with a flat top and covered in grass and creepers.

At the foot of the building we stopped and surveyed it.

'Wonder what it is?' said W.

'Looks like a mausoleum,' I murmured. Under the trailing bindweed that hung down the side I could see old carving on the stone wall.

'Mausoleum—out here, all on its own? Surely the Haggertons would have their family vault in the church crypt or whatever?'

'Whatever,' I said. 'It doesn't matter really. It's a lookout point for us. Tell you what, let's check it out now and come back with binos at the weekend. Right?'

'Right.' He looked up the wall. 'No hand holds that I can see.'

'Get off,' I retorted and grappling among the creeper vines I began to clamber up the wall. I landed back on the ground with a crash, my hands full of torn off bindweed. Winterbottom averted his eyes but could not conceal his superior smirk, while offering me a helping hand, which naturally I ignored and scrambled up.

'Look,' I told him, 'you're lighter. You get up on my back, get a grip on the parapet, then when you're on top you can give me a hand.'

He shook his head violently. My suggestion had offended the natural order of things in his eyes. He turned his back to the wall, laced his hands and fingers together, and said, 'Put your foot on and I'll hoist you up.'

There was no point arguing, but it was a big, big mistake. Or should I say, the firm of Prescot and Winterbottom had hit a bad, bad day.

My size eights were safely in his grasp and I rose splendidly up the creeper-clad wall, till my hands gripped the stone top. But, just as I was about to make the surge which would take my body over the edge, I heard W. gasp.

'Je-sus!'

My foot-support being removed, I fell to earth. As I slid down, my skirt, already fashionably split, slid up revealing all. At the same time, under my overwhelming weight, Winterbottom collapsed, while I fell on top of him in the bracken, still thus exposed, all in a split second.

Viewed from the rear—so to speak—it must have looked like one of those scenes from ancient mythology . . . 'Raid by Amazons' or such. The un-amusing thing about it was that it *was* viewed from the rear.

'Ahem,' said this voice.

I tried to adjust my garments, take the crushing weight off Sherlock, and look round. I managed all three. There stood Ms Courtney—who else? Silently she beckoned us. We scrambled to our feet and silently followed her. Neither questions nor answers seemed to meet the needs of the moment.

Ms Courtney led the way through the undergrowth. I now saw that we were following a sort of path I had not noticed before. It led in a roundabout way to the old iron gate. As we approached, as if by magic, the gamekeeper, gaiters and all, appeared, key in hand to let us out. He responded to Ms Courtney's gracious nod with a smile that I felt was overly familiar. A stray thought crossed my mind but vanished as we passed out into the Clough and Ms Courtney began to speak.

'Well, Emmeline, James. You know that the estate, even more than the Clough, is out of bounds . . . so . . . '

She paused and gave me what seemed to be a knowing smile. 'Shall I assume you were there for the usual reasons . . . ?'

At her words, Winterbottom actually hung his head and averted his glance. I, having too little experience of the depth of his deviousness, took his actions too literally. 'Don't be ridiculous!' I exploded. My remarks were really directed at him, but Ms Courtney took them as intended for her.

'I see,' she said grimly. 'If we weren't here in the undergrowth for that reason, shall I take it this means you were, despite our discussion this morning, still pursuing your investigations?'

Neither of us answered a word, but he shot me a poignant glance which said all too clearly, 'You idiot.' For once I felt he was right.

We had reached the wall of the science block by now. Ms Courtney produced a key and we passed through down the corridors and so out into the school yard. 'I suppose,' said Ms C., 'I ought to see you off the premises, but I think you will have got the message by now. Get off home. But we shall have words about this again.'

In silence, Winterbottom and I walked along the road. I waited for him to give me a rebuke for shooting my mouth off, but instead he turned to me in his Sherlock mode.

'The question is, what was she doing on the estate?'

I shrugged. 'Maybe she saw us go in and followed. Usual reasons.'

He ignored my suggestion, although his cheek went a shade pinker. 'Then why was she coming out rather than going in?'

I stared at him. 'How do you know which direction

she was heading when you were buried in clothing under bracken?'

'I was observing things as I fell,' he answered, straight-faced.

'Oh,' I answered. Other words failed me.

13 *James*

We were left to stew for a few days, expecting all the time to be called in to Ms Courtney, or even to the Boss, but all the time disappointed. It was all designed to wear us down, no doubt, and what was more bizarre, although we were careful not to meet behind the bike sheds or anywhere else, or even to talk to one another, I had the feeling we were being watched.

Prescot was being dogged by Natalie who I suppose was just on the look out for dirt,[7] while Dean Scully had his eye on me. The strange thing was—Dean Scully being what he was—there was no sign of him trying to get his own back. He just seemed to want to know what I was up to. Did he/Scully actually believe I was working with the police? The thought made me warm up under the collar. I was a sleuth not an informer. That was not agreeable to

[7] The story circulating was that we were due to be expelled for unspeakable doings in the bracken.—E. P.

me at all. Nor indeed, to the powers-that-be, as I found out later that week.

We were called in to Ms Courtney's office again, and there, next to her, with her, behind the desk was none other than DI Sharp. Q: Did they often have these tête-à-têtes?

DI Sharp murmured: 'Ah, the odd couple.' Ms Courtney, who was clearly in no mood for pleasantry, told us to sit down and opened fire. 'I thought, Emmeline, James, that you might begin to take my warnings seriously if I asked Detective Inspector Sharp to speak to you.'

DI Sharp looked at Prescot, then at me. 'I'm all for the public taking an interest in our work, and helping where we think it is appropriate. But we do not find it funny when amateur detectives, no matter how well meaning, start their own misdirected investigations.'

I moved my ankle out of range of Prescot's toe, and spoke firmly. 'Surely what we have been doing supplements the police work.'

He seemed to be grinding his teeth. Ms Courtney's eyebrows rose. Sharp concentrated his interview-room gaze on me.

'So far you have done the following: a) Persuaded Mrs Crowther that her son has taken off for good on a drugging spree; b) Persuaded Mrs Hardy that we are employing you to spy on them; c) Intruded on the private estate of a *media* [he weighed down on that word] personality, by implication linking him and his home with the disappearance of Adam and Amelia.'

My mind went into overdrive as I prepared a point-by-point answer to this rubbish, but Sharp hadn't finished.

'Can you imagine what would be the result if the press and television got hold of all this? We are already, naturally enough, in the spotlight. The police always are when kids—young people—go missing.'

I shifted my ground mentally. Prescot was clearly keeping quiet. So I said diplomatically, 'Inspector, I understand your concerns. Isn't it time for us to put the cards on the table and pool our findings?'

Ms Courtney's eyes were opening wider. DI Sharp's lips had suddenly grown very thin. I could see Prescot's foot edging towards me and moved my foot away. Sharp said, between his teeth, 'What findings?'

I knew this was the opening I had waited for: 'We think that the Haggerton Estate is very relevant to the search for Adam and Amelia.'

'Why?'

'Because the dosser—because Toby—came out of there, and went back in there.'

'And disappeared from there, as dossers do all the time. They shift around . . . ' said Sharp.

'He disappeared for a better reason than that, Inspector,' I answered triumphantly, 'because Toby wasn't a dosser— he was someone pretending to be a dosser—an *actor*.' (I emphasized the word.)

'So you're saying Cameron Hayter, one of the country's top show business people, was pretending to be a wino to throw the police off the scent?'

'Well, somebody was,' I insisted.

'How do you know this Toby wasn't a dosser?'

This was the moment I'd waited for. 'Because his eyes were all wrong. They weren't a wino's eyes. They were—'

'And you know all about alkies' eyes, do you, Jim lad?' Sharp shot at me.

This was the question I thought would come.

'I'm not in a position to discuss that right now but

I'm sure Toby was a phoney . . . ' I decided not to go any further.

Sharp took a deep breath. 'Listen, my lad. Detectives in fiction are allowed to have hunches like that, 'cause the author's on their side. In real life we have to find facts for theories. And there is nothing to make the police think Adam and Amelia's disappearance has anything to do with Cameron Hayter and the Haggerton Estate, with drugs and the Hardy family, or anything other than the usual reasons why young people go missing from home.'

'But how can you be so sure?'

DI Sharp shot a glance at Ms Courtney then said, 'The press will be told today, so I see no harm in letting you know. The Crowthers and Mrs Hardy have had letters from Newcastle—letters written by Adam and Amelia saying they are well and have gone away to think about their lives. We've taken time to check the letters are authentic, the parents are a little less worried now, and we have a new focus for our enquiries which,' he said slowly, 'will continue without your help, thank you very much.'

I looked at Prescot—she was still saying nothing. I opened my lips to speak but Sharp got in first. 'Read my lips, both of you. You are off this case.'

Ms Courtney tapped on her desk. 'Emmeline, James, I must add a word or two. The school also has its image to consider and its discipline. This is the second warning you have had from me. There will not be a third. If there are any more incidents, we shall be in touch with your parents and suspension—at the very least—will follow. Now you can go. Thank you.'

As we got into the corridor I turned to Prescot. 'You didn't say anything. What got into you?'

She looked at me: 'Do you reckon anything you said helped? No, we've got to do some heavy thinking. Right now I'm due for practice.' And off she strode.

14 Emmeline

Winterbottom and I did not speak for several days after that. I was bothered by two thoughts, neither of them comforting. One was—after the interview in Ms Courtney's office—had I got myself involved with an idiot who couldn't keep his mouth shut? The other was—did I keep my mouth shut because I didn't have the bottle (as Hardy might say) to speak out like he did?

I told myself that the real difference between me and him was that I was realistic enough to accept that Adam and Amelia were hiding in Newcastle if they hadn't stowed away on a boat to Valparaiso. Whereas Winterbottom clung to his theory that they were being held at Haggerton Hall—because 'Toby's eyes were wrong'. He wouldn't say how he could be so positive about that, which I found intriguing, but baffling. What do you do when your 'partner' in investigation provides you with another mystery?

I decided to get on with my life. The quarter finals for the District Cup loomed and there is nothing like thundering down the pitch to the ripe sound of splintering ankle bones to clear the mind of worries. I did see Winterbottom once on the touchline, his dark, penetrating gaze fixed on the sky. But it was a fleeting glimpse. Then the English Department wanted me to polish my essay about Great-gran and the suffragettes—for possible publication somewhere. And that was a distraction from detection.

Once or twice I saw him from afar, leaning, back to the wall, reading a battered copy of *The Sign of Four*, or simply staring straight ahead. If he saw me in the crowd, he gave no sign.

Then the school was knocked out of the cup. 'You're not concentrating, Em,' moaned Ms Frazer. My essay was polished and handed in. I was at a loose end.

I was missing something in my life—but what? Those bad-tempered sessions behind the bike sheds, the excitement of encounters with parents, illicit forays into the wilds of Haggerton Hall? Was I suffering withdrawal symptoms for the sound of Winterbottom's irritating, pompous, but sometimes astonishingly logical, comments? What was certain—life was duller.

Leaving school one day I saw him on the other side of the road. I crossed and fell into step beside him (which nearly did my knee joints in).

Without more ado I invited him round to our place for a quiet chat about where we were with the case (there was no sign yet, incidentally, of the fugitives being found in Newcastle), since we couldn't meet up at school without exciting rumour or comment. He was silent for a while, head bent, then suddenly said, 'Yeah, why not?' At which I nearly withdrew the invitation, but restrained myself. So next evening he came round. We sat in father's library and chatted for a while.

We did not get very far with the case—there was not a lot to go on but old data and theories. But that was not the only problem. The library is like one of those cottage-shaped barometers, where a woman and a man take turns to pop in and out.

First came Ma bearing plates of buns and orange juice for some idle chatter and a good look at Winterbottom at the same time. Then came Pa, noisy and looming as always, not engaging in idle chatter but, as usual, delivering a speech.

'Do you play rugger, Jim (I may call you Jim?)—no? Obviously can't stand sport from the look on your face— flannelled fools and muddied oafs, eh?'

'Oh, stop it, Dad!' I cried.

'What? James and I understand one another. We're mutually reactive types. I'm the complete philistine, he's an obvious intellectual—he's the keen reader type . . . ' Pa blundered on while Winterbottom sat po-faced. 'Bet you haven't many books at home, eh? Can tell by the way you look at the shelves. Life's all wrong, people who love books often can't afford 'em—and you have idiots who buy books by the yard . . . '

Pa gave him a disabling punch on the shoulder and said, 'You come round any time you like and have a read—borrow 'em if you like—we know where you live, ho ho! No one'll bother you—not even our Margaret.'

I saw Winterbottom's eyebrows go up when he heard 'Margaret'. Pa ploughed on.

'She hardly ever comes in here. The only book she's interested in is her blessed great-gran's diary—and she'd keep that in her own room if I let her—but I put my foot down. I won't bother you either, Jim lad. All I ever need is my books of sermons—you know, if it's Lent, it's self-denial; if it's Christmas, it's peace and goodwill—the usual old toffee . . . '

At last I could stand it no longer.

'Pa! Stop showing off. James isn't impressed!'

Winterbottom blinked. I'd never used his first name before—but you can't bring anyone home on whatever pretext and keep using their surname.

Pa roared. 'Listen to that, Jim. She's a born bully. Don't let her bully you or you're a lost soul.' I saw a quick gleam come into Winterbottom's eye then vanish again. What he might have been thinking of, I can't imagine.

Ma and Pa at last left us in peace, but Winterbottom did not hang about—for which I was grateful. There was not much more we could discuss and both of us were embarrassed.

But as he left I saw him give a lingering glance at the bookshelves.

15 *James*

'Well, Jim, you'll have to invite her round, won't you?'

My mouth fell open. 'Get off, Mum. You're joking.'

'You're forced to, lad.'

'Why?'

'You have to return hospitality—at least, in my book you do.'

'Hospitality?' I stared at Mum. 'Two buns and a glass of orange juice.'

She shrugged. 'That's the way they do things at the vicarage, I expect. We do it differently. Invite her round to tea.'

I knew what Mum meant by tea—enough food to sink a ship.

'Oh no, Mum.' I made a last protest.

'What's up with you, lad?'

I could feel my face going red. 'She'll think . . . I want to like . . . get in with her.'

'Well, don't you?'

'No!'

'There's no need to shout, lad—it always gives the opposite impression.'

'Mum—it's just common interests—intellectual affinity.'

'Oh, that's what they call it these days, is it?' She paused. 'Come on, lad. I want to have a look at the vicar's daughter.'

I breathed deeply and said no more. But I felt things were getting out of control. Mum had no idea what this particular vicar's daughter was like. For a day or two I cherished the hope that Prescot would say no or make some excuse.

No such luck. There she sat at our table, facing Mum across a mountain range of pies, ham, tuna sandwiches, home-made cakes, enough for a funeral tea. I guessed I'd be eating this for days after. Another notion I had was that they wouldn't be able to talk to one another—and if they did they'd fall out. I was wrong and right at the same time.

Prescot noshed as if there was no tomorrow. Maybe they starved her at home. And she and Mum rabbited on as if I wasn't there. Any efforts I made to turn the conversation to other matters were totally disregarded.

They went at it hammer and tongs all about women and equality. Prescot's voice rose, Mum's got sharper. I began to think about sneaking out.

'Working women, I'll tell you something about working women. They're mostly madams,' said Mum. 'Give 'em an inch and they'll take a yard.'

'Ah,' retorted Prescot, 'that's because they've never been given a chance to show their potential—men stand in their way all the time.'

Mum laughed—I've never heard her laugh as loudly as that.

'I'll take you down to Meredith's where I work, sometime, and show you how they plague the men charge-hands and overseers—especially the new young ones. When they're all together they make their lives a misery—when they're on their own and think the others can't see, they play up to them. I tell you, Emmeline—men are self-satisfied and pompous, but women are devious and scheming.'

'Ah, but if they were equal, they wouldn't have to scheme.'

'No, they'd be self-satisfied and pompous, I expect.'

To my utter astonishment they looked at each other and burst into shrieks of laughter. I shrugged and got on with eating everything that Prescot hadn't already guzzled.

A couple of hours later as she was leaving and we stood together in our tiny hall, Prescot said to me, 'Your mum's terrific. You're lucky.'

There was no answer to that, so I changed the subject. 'Are we going to meet up again? To discuss the case,' I added quickly in case she got the wrong idea.

She gave me a sharp glance. 'What is there to discuss? Either Adam and Hardy are up north or they're hidden in Haggerton Hall.'

'They're in the Hall.' I tried to speak firmly. She wasn't impressed.

'You know? Just because you say that dosser's eyes are all wrong. But you won't tell me how you're so sure.'

'I can't tell you, just now . . . '

She wasn't having that. Her voice rose.

'You mean we're partners but you're keeping secrets from me.'

I looked round, alarmed, and put my fingers to my lips. I could hear Mum singing in the kitchen.

'It's just . . . private,' I whispered, all the time wishing I'd kept my mouth shut about Toby's eyes.

At the word 'private' her ginger eyebrows rose. 'Oh, like that, eh.'

As the front door closed behind her there was a gleam in her eye that should have warned me.

Those were the last words we spoke together about the Adam/Hardy investigation for many days. In the meantime, I'm sorry to say, Prescot and I got diverted into the business of investigating . . . each other.

16 *James*

I did go back to the vicarage library but it was not because the Revd Prescot urged me to. To tell the truth I was wary of meeting Prescot's father again. I don't like being preached at by a heavyweight boxer while he dislocates my shoulder with his fist and calls me 'Jim lad', like some refugee from *Treasure Island*.

Mrs Prescot seemed OK—even if her idea of refreshment wasn't on the scale of my mum's—but you couldn't tell, because between the father and the daughter she never seemed to get a word in edgeways—just fluttered in and out with a tray, giving quick glances round like a bird.

No, what drew me like a magnet was the sight, above the rows of dark brown leather-bound sermons, of something else—pure gold in my eyes. It was a row of bound volumes of *Strand Magazine* of a hundred years ago—just the time when the first Sherlock Holmes stories were coming out, the ones with the old illustrations. Just thinking about them made me drool.

So one evening after school I went there. I rang on the bell, and nearly turned away when I heard him booming away on the other side of the front door. It was flung open and there he stood, his great beefy paw held out. I goggled. He stared. Then he roared with laughter.

'Why, it's Jim lad. I thought you were some idiot coming about marriage arrangements. Ho ho. They won't get you that easily, will they? Come in, come in.'

His hand on my back flung me down the passage, while he bellowed, 'Stella, Margaret, look who's here!'

Before I could think or look round, I was propelled round the corner and in through the library door where the smell of books was like a fog. But just as I crossed the doorway, I saw out of the corner of my eye a head of wild, red hair sticking out above the landing rail. Prescot was in but though I stayed for an hour, she did not come down. In a way I was relieved because to be honest there was nothing new to talk over about the case and I wasn't quite sure of myself on other topics of conversation with her.

Her mother was different, though. As soon as Pa had flung me into a very comfy leather armchair and obligingly handed me down one of the *Strand Magazines*, in she came with two buns and a plate and a glass of juice. They must have a strict regime in that house.

She smiled at me, put down the plate, and then, perching herself on the arm of another chair, she began to chat. At first I was a bit peeved because I really wanted to get stuck into 'A Scandal in Bohemia' (the page had fallen open at that one). But there was something in her face that made me rest the book on my knee and listen. I forget what we talked about—maybe family, school, hobbies, the normal stuff.

It was only later on when I went home and was lying on my bed thinking about it that I realized what had been going on. She'd have made a good detective because in between all the idle chatter she slipped questions, which I answered without thinking.

On that visit and the next couple of evenings I ran through 'The Red-Headed League', 'The Speckled Band', 'Silver Blaze', 'The Final Problem', and was looking forward to *The Hound of the Baskervilles*.

Mrs P. was doing well too because she'd got through my entire family history—where Mum worked, what happened to my father, what I planned to do when I left school, and loads of other classified information, including a bit about Prescot's and my investigation. Though there, out of professional loyalty, I didn't reveal anything significant. I began to have a suspicion I was being pumped about what her daughter was doing when not playing hockey.

But then something happened. It was quite by chance that reaching up the shelves (the *Strand Mags* were above my head level) with nothing more than 'The Adventure of Black Peter' in mind, I noticed a yellow-backed volume with the word 'Journal' on the spine.

Something made me pick it out and sit down with it. I realized in a moment it was no ordinary book because it was hand-written in ink that had turned brown, while the pages were beginning to crumble and fray at the edges.

The name inside the front cover, Emmeline Huxtable, told me all. It was Great-grandmother's diary.

At first I read idly, just opening it here and there, but it wasn't long before I was hooked. It was gripping stuff—if you left on one side all her long tirades about men and how inferior they were, how God had made a mistake doing Adam first when the other way round was clearly nature's way. But when she wrote about the exploits of her hockey team, or her adventures at rallies— fighting with the police, umbrellas and handbags swinging, periods in prison—that was so exciting I had to read it page by page.

Then the tone changed. She'd met someone—someone who knocked her over. The entries got shorter and shorter, scrappier and scrappier as though it was all too private even for her diary . . . It seemed to be coming to some kind of crunch, then quite suddenly there was a gap.

I turned the page quickly. At the top was written: ' . . . my family will have to accept that I shall have this child and bring it up without a father . . . '

Then there was no more, just blank, faded paper.

There was something strange about that page I'd turned. I fingered it, my mind ticking over. But what it was I couldn't work out. I held the page up to the light. I could just make out some sort of words, back to front. But before I could take it in I was interrupted.

I heard a noise, looked up, and was astounded to see Prescot standing there, with her hand held out. She wasn't looking friendly. I got up hastily, muttering, 'I was just going to put this back.'

'Don't bother,' she said. 'I'll take it upstairs, thank you.' That 'thank you' was said in the sort of tone you use when you mean the opposite.

Prescot's voice is like her dad's. It carries. And who should appear in the doorway but the Revd himself?

'That's no way to speak to a gentleman—even if that is against your principles. But I suppose manners go out of the window where that precious diary's concerned, eh, Margaret?'

I thought Prescot was going to burst into flames. 'You know I hate that name,' she snapped and turning round she charged from the room, with him calling after her.

'It's the one you were christened with, my dear.'

He turned to me and spread out his hands.

'Sorry, Jim lad. But you know what they're like. Just take no notice.'

For some reason I can't fathom I had an impulse to say to him: 'Why don't you leave her alone. If she wants to call herself Emmeline or Ermintrude, it's her own business.'

But I didn't. I just gave a silly grin, excused myself, and went home. The fact was my mind was hard at work. That diary and Prescot's almost open anger because I'd been looking through it. I'd stumbled on something—a mystery that nagged at me as the days went by.

I'd have been better off concentrating on the Adam/ Hardy mystery, even if that was a dead end. For I was not to know where that diary would lead me.

I kept away from Prescot's place for a couple of days. I was embarrassed. There's only one thing more embarrassing than seeing someone your own age told off by their parents, and that's having them see *you* being told off.

But I went back, all the same. There were two novels and nearly thirty short stories I hadn't read through. (Of course I'd read them before, but not in the original mag.) And that *diary* fascinated me—though I didn't expect to find it in the library any more. I was sure Prescot had taken it up to her room—what I'd been witness to was just another round in the battle with the powers-that-be.

I must be quite frank, though. The final push that sent me back to Prescot's library was coming home from school one late afternoon to hear voices from our front room—with the clatter of plates and cups. At first I thought Mum was gossiping with somebody from work, but no, I recognized the other voice all too well. It was my ex-partner-in-detection having a heart-to-heart, woman-to-woman chat with Mum.

I put my jacket back on, closed the front door quietly behind me and walked round to the vicarage.

It was Mrs Prescot who let me in, with that little smile of hers.

'Why, James, do come in. I'm just having tea on my own. Relaxing after the Mother's Union meeting. Would you like a cup before you settle down with old Sherlock?'

I realized I wasn't intended to say 'no', so I didn't. I followed her, not into their sitting room, but into the kitchen where the table was stacked with crockery.

'Excuse all this, James. I'll just clear a corner. I love to have my tea in here, the afternoon sun comes through the window.'

I sat down near the sink. I felt comfortable. Kitchens are the most comfortable rooms in the house, really. I heard her shut the door. The kettle whistled, saucers rattled, and there we were sitting with our teacups perched on the draining board. She smiled at me again, then put a hand on my sleeve.

'I wanted to have this little chat with you, James. We don't get much of a chance in the library with father and . . . Emmeline, barging about. Oh dear, I shouldn't say it but I hate that name Emmeline. I think Margaret's such a lovely name. I wouldn't have minded her insisting on Peggy, but Emmeline. Don't you think so? Tell me, you seem close to her . . . '

I shrugged, feeling my face beginning to warm up. It was time, I felt, for me to wheel out the 'intellectual affinity' bit, but I hesitated too long (though thinking about it afterwards, I doubt it would have made any difference). Mrs Prescot went on.

'I'm afraid any boy who likes Margaret is on a beating to nothing. I don't know whether it's in her nature, or whether it's just a passing phase. I just wish she would be a more . . . average girl . . . you know, have a boyfriend and be nice to him.'

The idea of Prescot being 'nice' gave me a strange feeling. I had to turn and look out of the window so Mrs P. wouldn't see my face. But she got hold of the wrong end of the stick. Back went her hand on my sleeve.

'I'm sorry, James, to be so blunt. But I think you are a sensitive, intelligent boy and you don't deserve to be hurt.'

I slid off my chair. I shook hands with her desperately, gabbled something about 'thanks for the tea', and made tracks for the door. As I went I was mourning for *The Valley of Fear*, *His Last Bow*, and a dozen other Holmes stories. But I knew I wasn't going to set foot in that library again—at least not until I had sorted certain things out, about my connection with Prescot.

That wasn't all, for during that conversation with Mrs P. I had suddenly realized what it was that was strange about those last pages in Emmeline Huxtable's diary. It told me a lot I didn't know about Prescot. It almost made me feel sorry for her in a way. But what her mother had told me about her put other thoughts in my mind. Yes, I certainly needed a sort out with Prescot and the sooner the better. The question was how, where, and when.

As I came in through the front door at home Mum was siding away dishes.

'Oh, there you are, Jim. Your girlfriend was here for tea. She's a funny one, but she's a nice kid underneath.'

Words failed me.

17 Emmeline

I t was not envisaged—no, I'll start again, it was not imagined, that Winterbottom would get under my skin. Irritate me, yes, with his unbearable pomposity, amuse me with his total lack of a sense of humour, embarrass me with his inability to keep his mouth shut at crucial moments, and very occasionally impress me with his unusual knowledge—but getting under my skin is something I did not allow for.

Indeed when he succeeded I realized in a flash of insight which came too late (my 'intuition' let me down) that I should never have let him past the door of our house. I totally underestimated his ability—or should I say capacity, because I'm sure he didn't know what he was doing—to completely destroy the balance I'd achieved in my dealings with Pa and Ma—i.e., they left me alone.

On the other hand maybe Pa outwitted me (or was it Ma by putting the idea into Pa's head?) by inviting W.

with his ferret's nose into the library at home where like the book-maniac he so thoroughly is, not content with Sherlock Holmes he would in the end lay his hands on Emmeline Huxtable and precipitate a whole family psycho-drama about me and my name. They'd been working for months to fall on me over that, and Winterbottom, blundering fool, gave them the chance.

I was certainly upset—and I will not underestimate by how much. But I caught a glance of his face as I flowed up the stairs and, though in a rage, I was still able to see that the whole scene was an education to him.

Tit-for-tat—maybe he, too, wished he'd never opened the door of his life to a fellow manic-detective.

For where does detection begin and end? It shouldn't start, like charity, at home, but it does—and it hurts.

I had to do something by way of a fight-back. And I had to talk to somebody—somebody who treated me as an equal, i.e., disagreed with me, but listened to me as well. There was only one candidate who filled those needs within the nearest square mile and that was Winterbottom's mum.

A couple of days later I flew out of school and shot across to his home, stopping at the shops en route and turning up at the door with a box of chocolates plus a bunch of flowers and a pretty speech saying thank you for the enormous tea she'd given me the other day.

Mrs W. was at home and welcomed me in. In no time she had the kettle on, the choc box was opened and dipped into again and again. Chocs and tea do not go together and I didn't care and neither did she.

After a little while she raised a finger. The front door was opening as her son came in from school but he went out again almost immediately. I sensed in my bones that he would head for the vicarage. Pa would be out, on purpose to avoid the Mother's Union, and Winterbottom would get tea and sympathy in the kitchen from Ma. I reckoned I'd get the better of the bargain.

I kicked off (I know that's the wrong game) by asking her whether she thought—as a case in point—it was right to change your name.

'You mean your surname or your first name?' she asked, which stopped me in my tracks. 'I mean you can do one legally (or you can get married like I did)—I drew a short straw with our Joe's name—bless him—still, I'm stuck with it and like to let people know Winterbottom doesn't bother me. But strictly speaking you're stuck with your first name—or your Christian name in your case—I mean, it's on your birth certificate—it'll be on your marriage certificate.'

'I shan't get married!'

'Early days . . . and it'll be on your death certificate.' She stopped, popped a choc in her mouth and chewed then said, 'What do you want to change to, then? I know Emmeline's a bit long and drawn out but people can call you Em!'

'No, no,' I protested. 'My real name—I mean my baptismal name—is Margaret.'

'Nowt wrong with that. But you prefer Emmeline. No accounting for taste.'

I plunged in and explained why 'Emmeline'. She listened while I ran on—it is rather a long story. Though now and then she smiled, and now and then she shook her head, not in a discouraging way but in a 'getaway!' way.

'And you do actually like Emmeline?' she said at last.

'Truly,' I said.

I must have spoken a little too forcefully for she said, 'That's OK, love. When it comes to the point it's what you get called, not what you're baptized that counts. I was christened Esmerelda, but my friends called me Trixie, which was a blessing.'

I stopped her then. 'Emmeline is not supposed to be a nickname. It's a sort of commitment to things I believe in.'

She looked at me, then nodded, said, 'I believe you,' then suddenly started off at a tangent. 'You won't let him down, will you?'

To say I was gob-smacked is putting it mildly. I think my mouth fell open. She hurried on, a bit confused.

'You see, he wants a good friend—no, I don't mean that—he needs a good friend . . .'

She actually turned a little red at this point, which helped me keep quiet, waiting for what might come next, I suppose.

'You see—how can I put it—our Jimmy doesn't reckon much to the fellows he knows and he's scared of girls.'

'He doesn't seem scared of me,' I burst out.

'Ah well—you're not a girl, are you—'

Her hand went to her mouth, then she reached out and touched my arm.

'No, I'm sorry, that sounds awful, doesn't it? But I mean you're not a girlie girl, are you? That's what he's really scared of, the ones he thinks are going to drip all over him. Like that one in the flats across the road—she's in your class at school—Natalie Whatsit—she hangs about when he goes to school in the morning—so he sneaks out the back way.'

I was about to say something—I'm not sure what—when she took my breath away.

'He thinks the world of you.'

She must have seen I didn't believe her so she went on, 'No, he doesn't actually say anything like that—but he talks about you, tells me things you've said . . . Don't get me wrong when I say friend—I just meant friend— someone you can talk to . . . someone you can rely on—I mean, does it matter who they are, boy or girl, as long as you can trust them?'

The right words were still out of my reach, when she said something that changed the whole run of our chat. 'He misses his dad an awful lot. They were good friends—once, when Jimmy was younger, before . . . things changed.'

She stopped as if she'd said too much. What had happened between Winterbottom and his father, that spoilt things? I spoke hastily.

'Yes—James [I didn't like using his first name but his surname was impossible] told me about his father drowning at sea . . . '

She gave me a funny look . . . 'At sea? He told you that, did he?' What did that mean? Suddenly I felt that awful pressing need to know that gets one into such difficult situations.

'When was it?' I asked.

'Seven years ago, this month. On the 23rd.' She looked across the room to the sideboard and I noticed for the first time the photograph in its frame, a man in a blue jacket with sharp blue eyes. It was an intelligent face but a sad one, I thought. Suddenly an idea struck me, not an idea so much as two queries rolled into one. I needed answers to them because they might give me a clue to something else that was puzzling me.

And I knew I could not ask her. I might be mistaken

and, if I were, I'd be in dead trouble. She was someone I did not want to upset—just when we'd become friendly, and could talk openly about all sorts of other matters.

'I'm sorry, Mrs Winterbottom.'

'You can call me Trixie, love.'

'I'm afraid I have to rush.'

'That's OK. We've had a good natter. Come round any time in the afternoon. I'm usually on the early turn, it suits me better.'

I left her and hurried away. It was just gone five. The library closed at six on Thursdays and there was something I had to look up, about W.'s father.

As I came into the Reference Room, something caught my eye—a big spread from the local paper on one of the reading stands. Pictures of Adam and Amelia stared out at me. I hurried across to read it.

But there was nothing new. Just an appeal for information . . . ' . . . have Adam and Amelia just become two of the nearly 20,000 registered missing persons in this country . . . ?'

No, I thought. But the powers-that-be are probably looking in the wrong place and there's nothing I or Winterbottom can do about that.

Then I remembered what I'd come to the library for and a few minutes later I was scrolling the screen for back numbers of the local paper—September seven years ago. I was looking for some kind of obituary for Joseph Winterbottom—a few remarks in a funeral report, anything that might throw a little more light on the questions in my mind. I wasn't so much hopeful as simply curious—I wanted to know more about Winterbottom's father—it would explain—it would help to explain . . .

I struck gold. All of a sudden, there it was, not in September, but early in October; not the obituary, but the *inquest* on Joseph Winterbottom, Merchant Marine, who died by drowning when . . . I read on, not thinking of him, but his son and what he had said and what he knew. I felt angry with him and sorry at the same time.

I felt a strong urge to talk to him, quietly on our own. And I knew what to do. I'd meet him at the weekend, I thought—we could go for a walk on the Clough—no one would hear what we said to each other and maybe things could be cleared up.

It didn't work out quite like that, however.

At lunch time next day, Yasmin, holding her latest novel with her finger still tucked in to mark the place, called me to one side.

'I've been meaning to tell you, Em. You are being talked about.'

'So what's new.'

'No, idiot, you and little Winterbottom. You're not making yourself ridiculous by any chance, are you?'

'What's that supposed to mean?'

'I leave aside tête-à-têtes behind the bike sheds—I mean, popping in and out of each other's homes.'

'What are you talking about?'

'You were seen going into their place with flowers yesterday.'

'Seen?' Light dawned. 'I'll strangle Natalie.'

'Good thinking, but hurry—because it'll soon be all round the school.'

Now I knew I *had* to talk to Winterbottom.

Emmeline and James

18

Walking on the Clough that Saturday afternoon was a good idea in one way because there was no one around to hear when voices were raised—as they were.

On the other hand, slipping down grassy slopes, jumping over streams, losing your shoes in bogs, struggling up again while getting extremely hot, does not help an intelligent discussion of a difficult problem, and that was needed.

The trouble was the other person's hang-ups made intelligent discussion impossible.

I tried to start it off calmly and, to clear the air, saying to Winterbottom, 'Let's get it straight. It is intellectual affinity, isn't it? I mean, like, nothing more than that?'

'What d'you mean?'

'I mean you're not going . . . stupid about me . . . ?'

'You must be out of your tiny mind.'

'Thank you.'

I tried to make it clear to Prescot.

'You actually think I fancy you? I'd hate to think you thought I fancied you. I wouldn't even like to think you thought, I thought you fancied me . . . '

'That's brilliantly clear!'

'I'll spell it out. It would worry me if you thought you were going to exploit our intellectual relationship to make some kind of ego-tripping feminist statement.'

'Who's out of their tiny mind now?'

Now we were getting to the nitty-gritty.

'Just because I'm friendly with your mother and happen to have talked a bit about you—and your problems—doesn't mean that—'

'I could say the same about you and your mother.'

'And what's that supposed to mean—what's she been saying about me?'

'I specifically didn't make any remarks about your mother, because I didn't want to embarrass you—but you started it.'

'I started what?'

'This business about me and my problems—which I haven't got, and if I did have I wouldn't need any help from a big-head like you.'

'You know what your problem is? You've got a good mind, but you've also got a chip on your shoulder as big as a plank.'

So far we'd only been sparring. I thought it was time I stopped her in her tracks. 'Our relationship was a meeting of minds, not an intellectual hockey pitch. Don't think you can walk all over me.'

'Don't flatter yourself. Look, the fact is, I'm not interested in you one tiny little bit.'

'What d'you mean?'

'I mean I'm not interested in whether you're interested—'

'That's a relief. I'd begun to think that intellectual affinity is an idea the female mind found impossible to grasp.'

'Rubbish—that's one thing I'm totally objective about: the relationship between the sexes.'

'Oh yeah? Then why did you glue those two pages together in your great-gran's diary?'

That did it. Prescot stopped, one foot in the stream, the other on the bank. Her face was white—her hair stood up as though she was on fire.

'What are you raving about?'

I turned and looked down at her. I could do this because I was higher up the slope. I spoke coldly and calmly.

'You glued those two pages together so you could carry on pretending Emmeline Huxtable wanted to have that baby on her own. But she didn't, the father walked out on her. You cut that vital sentence in two, didn't you? What it really said was "Hard as it is for me, I must accept, and my family must accept, that I shall bring this baby up on my own, without its father". But by gluing the two pages together you cut out the front ten words up to "my family" and made it sound quite different. D'you know how I knew?'

She gave me a withering look but said nothing. I went on.

'Because the "my family" was written with a small "m", not a capital letter. So I knew it was the middle of a sentence, not the beginning. And when I held the page up to the light I saw what you'd done.'

Prescot took a deep breath, then said very quietly, 'I

suppose that gave you a great deal of satisfaction finding that out.'

I shook my head. 'No, it didn't. I felt sorry for you—you were just kidding yourself. I didn't mean to say anything to you about it—but when you started being so bloody patronizing about me and what I thought about you . . . '

I'd had enough of this. I pulled my foot out of the water, scrambled up the bank until I was looking down.

'Oh, so I am kidding myself, am I? And what about you?'

'Me? I'm not kidding myself.'

'No?—Not kidding yourself about your father—"drowned at sea"?'

Dark eyes stood out in his face, the corners of his mouth went down.

'He was.'

'Oh, indeed, he was. He walked from the pub right off the quay at Fairmouth, out of his skull with booze.'

'Shut up!'

I should have done, but I didn't.

'That's how you knew ''Toby'' wasn't an alky. That's how you knew his eyes were all wrong, because you'd seen your father in that state too many times.'

'You're enjoying telling me all this, aren't you?' His voice shook.

'No I'm not, you idiot. I was sorry for you. I wouldn't have said anything about it, if you hadn't decided to play your little detective game on my private affairs and rub my nose in it.'

'Who's talking?'

'Anyway now we both know, don't we?'

'Yes, I know what sort of person you are.'

'Ditto!'

And that was it. We didn't say another word. We moved off smartly in opposite directions.

19   *Emmeline*

J ust when our partnership had gone bust the Adam–
Hardy case suddenly came to life—in the most
amazing way.

Ms Courtney called about a dozen of us together and
said, in a nonchalant sort of way, 'I've been having a word
with Cameron Hayter.'

'Oooh!' went the idiots in our number. She smiled
complacently.

'As a matter of fact I had been to the Hall to see
him—to offer the school's apologies for the intrusions into
his estate. [A likely story, I thought.] He was surprisingly
relaxed about it and said he would be happy to give a
guided tour of the Hall and grounds to a select group,
and—' she looked quickly in my direction, '—he even
included any intruders in the invitation. I think he
believes this might cure them. I hope he's right.'

'Will we be able to talk to him?' gasped one of the
idiots.

'Of course,' said Ms Courtney, but went on severely, 'but not pester him. Understood?'

So, the next day, we arrived at Haggerton Hall in the school bus. Now I saw it at close hand, I realized that it was not all that old—maybe a hundred years or so: there was a lot of red-brick. But inside it was suitably grand, with all the standard stately-home features: sweeping staircase, chandeliers, enormous picture gallery with all the Haggertons from the past glaring down at you.

We were taken into a drawing room where staff in uniform served us refreshments. I could not resist doing my Miss Marple bit and asked one of the waitresses a question. She looked blank, then said, 'Oh, I wouldn't know. We're from the town, outside caterers. They don't run to permanent staff much, I'm told. The cleaning people and kitchen staff come in early morning, do their thing and go.'

'There's a gamekeeper . . . ' I remembered.

She chuckled. 'Oh, him—he's a jack of all trades, him . . . ' and she said no more. But what she'd told me had set my sleuthing instincts working again. Without thinking I looked round for Winterbottom, but he was pointedly staring out of the window at something.

A tall thin man in a dark suit came in and beckoned us to follow him through the Hall while he did the guide bit. I was right about the age. 'Smart of you to spot it, miss.' He cleared his throat and raised his voice. 'Haggerton Hall in its present form dates from 1820, though built upon foundations which go back to the fourteenth century.'

He led the way up the stairs. 'This staircase dates from

the late sixteenth century, miraculously surviving almost intact the disastrous fire of 1817, which destroyed most of the earlier building.'

Stopping us by a large window, he pointed outwards. 'All that is left of the original battlements. Severely damaged during the Wars of the Roses, in which the Haggertons changed sides twice, but lost out each time, the original fortifications were finally levelled to the ground by one of Cromwell's colonels. The family fortunes revived in the early eighteenth century when the twelfth Lord Haggerton's privateering ventures brought in enormous wealth, mainly in Spanish gold.

'Easy come, easy go, as they say, the thirteenth Lord Haggerton (an appropriate number) wasted the substance in living and deeds so riotous that he is said to have inspired those aristocrats who later formed the Hell Fire Club.

'The fourteenth and fifteenth Lords Haggerton restored what the thirteenth had lost by investing in coal mining and canals. The abandoned shafts at Haggerton Clough still remain to mark their ventures—as does the present Hall.'

With this he led us out on to a huge balcony overlooking the grounds, which stretched away, gardens and spinneys and bracken, to the old stone wall Winterbottom and I had climbed what now seemed years ago. Behind my shoulder I suddenly heard his sharp voice asking, 'What's that . . . ruin . . . right over near the wall with all the grass growing over it?'

'Ah, that is the tomb of the thirteenth Lord Haggerton himself.'

'Isn't it a bit big for a grave?'

The guide smiled. 'It is rumoured that the building

was used for his more private orgies. When he died he left instructions that his body should be placed inside, presumably so he could continue his enjoyments privately in the after life.'

'What did he die of?'

'Ah—that is a moot question. A little to the west—or shall we say left of the tomb—hidden by the woods, is a small dark pool on the edge of the woods.'

'How deep is it? Deep enough to drown in?'

'A good question. It is reputed to be bottomless and to be swarming with pike so big that they could snap off a man's arm.'

This ridiculous statement got a shudder from the idiots. Encouraged, the guide went on. 'The pool is also allegedly haunted by the thirteenth Lord who drowned there. His clothes were found on the bank. Some suggested he had drowned himself in a fit of remorse, some that his son the fourteenth Lord had him murdered in order to save the estate. But local folklore has it that the Evil One in the form of a giant pike dragged him into the depths when, still drunk after one of his feasts, he incautiously went for a swim at midnight.'

I was getting a little tired of the oohs and ahs and so changed the subject. 'What's the bigger building, closer to the Hall?'

The guide gave me a condescending smile. 'Ah, that is the tithe barn, certainly fifteenth century, possibly fourteenth.'

'Could we have a look over it?' I asked.

'Ah,' he answered gravely, 'we must ask . . . ' he paused as if wishing he could say 'his Lordship', then went on, 'the present owner for permission.'

Down we trooped to the ground floor and as we

gathered in the drawing room and more refreshments were pressed on us, in walked the great man Cameron Hayter himself, taller than me(!), broad and handsome (if you care for the embroidered-shirt-half-unbuttoned-over-hairy-chest-type). He made us a little speech of welcome and asked if we had seen all we wanted.

Before I could get in my request Winterbottom, who was evidently intrigued by a nearby room, started to ask him questions about that. When at last I got my word in, Hayter declared grandly that the guide could conduct one party round the tithe barn, while he did the honours indoors.

The tithe barn was empty, with huge whitewashed walls, and massive blackened beams like ship's timbers holding up the roof. The guide was pointing out the various features and dating them when I spotted something that made me go hot and cold with excitement.

The wall at one end seemed to cut off part of the roof beams, putting it out of balance with the other end. Part of the barn had been walled off at some point in time, I was sure, but if it were a partition wall I could see no door in it. I took a fix from a small window up near the roof beams then quickly stepped outside. I'd struck gold. The outside wall must be two metres longer than the inside. There was an enclosed space there, not big, but a secret chamber of sorts. The guide made no mention of it and I didn't like to ask—this was something I needed to mull over.

'Ah, Emmeline, what are you investigating now?' Ms Courtney stood behind me.

'Nothing, Ms Courtney,' I said with downcast eye. 'I felt a bit funny so I came outside for fresh air.'

It was a wild invention but it served its purpose. I

was left alone to think about my discoveries. I needed to talk it over with someone, only I wasn't talking to the someone, was I . . .

20 *James*

I t seemed bizarre. All that history—all those earls and lords—and now Haggerton Hall was just home for a soap star. But wasn't Cameron Hayter a little bit more than a soap star? And wasn't I here to keep my eyes open for any clues to what he *was* up to—if my theory was correct and he was linked to Adam and Hardy's disappearance?

So I kept my critical thoughts to myself and looked around me all the time while listening with half an ear to this old bloke droning on about the tenth Lord and the eighteenth and so forth. Prescot, who went in front all the time, seemed to be all ears and intelligent questions about the history of the place. She'd obviously stopped thinking about the case we'd once been working on together, so it was down to me to keep that investigation going.

Still, I must admit that when we got out on the balcony, and saw in the distance that old grass-covered ruin we'd tried to climb up, and heard about the dark little pool nearby, I found I wanted to know more about the man whose bones were supposed to be lying under the stones. Not that the old wives' tale the guide trotted out added much worthwhile to my knowledge but that pool by the trees stayed in my mind even after the visit was over.

And my mind zoomed back to the investigation the moment we got downstairs. For I spotted through a half-closed door leading off the room where we were being fed and watered, another office-like place that was wall-to-wall computers. All the very latest gear. It was like a spaceship.

The moment I asked to have a look inside, Cameron Hayter seemed to become wary. But he gave the old professional smile and said:

'OK, I'll show one or two of you round, on the strict understanding that it is look and not touch.' He laughed, a bit too heartily, I thought. 'I don't want my scripts shooting into a black hole.'

'Ooh,' gasped one of the fan club, 'do you learn your parts electronically?'

'Ah no. This is a television serial I'm writing—a career change.'

'Ooh—what's it about?'

'Ah, that's a secret. But I can give you an idea—it's about someone who wants to sabotage the plans to grow GM crops, by using the Net to mobilize all the eco-warriors in the country, and how the government and big business try to track them down.'

'Ooh, does he get caught?'

'Ho ho. You'll have to wait till it's screened to find out, I'm afraid. I don't even know myself.'

While all this chat was going on my eyes were roving here and there. And suddenly, I couldn't believe what I saw. Right in the centre of the room were two identical computers on separate stands, like dual controls in an aircraft—pilot and co-pilot. And perched on the very corner of one of them was a little oddly shaped chunk of green plastic—no bigger than an eraser. But I knew it wasn't.

When I saw out of the corner of my eye that Hayter's head was turned while he answered the fan's questions I flicked the green thing off the computer. It shot into a corner and I leapt across and whipped it off the floor and into my pocket.

My movement must have caught his eye for as I straightened up I found him looking at me.

'Found something, kid?' he asked very casually.

I was equally casual. 'Nah, just dropped my eraser, sir.'

He nodded, gave me another searching glance, then turned away. But as our eyes met, I was sure of one thing. I was looking at 'Toby'.

As we left Haggerton Hall on the school bus I was certain I was on the trail of Adam and Hardy again.

Adam at least was around the Hall. He was working on some computer project with Cameron Hayter—maybe that eco-warrior film. But why should that be so hush-hush—why should Adam be in hiding and (here my mind went into overdrive), why did he leave a chunk of his mascot for me to find? I was positive he'd done that on purpose.

Why, why? I needed to talk it over with someone, but . . .

21 Emmeline

My mind was in a stew that week—a stew with different ingredients. I was furious with Winterbottom for what he'd done to me over Great-gran's diary, though I know the fury was partly because what he'd said was true. I was alarmed in case it all got back to my parents (supposing he had another cosy kitchen chat with Ma?). I felt a fool—I felt in his power. But somewhere in the simmering mess was the sight of his face when I told him I knew the truth about his father. Only will-power stopped him crying there in front of me on the Clough.

Then there was frustration. That tour of Haggerton Hall, the discovery I'd made about the tithe barn. If Adam and Hardy were being held on the Haggerton Estate then a pound to a penny they were in that secret chamber, while we were walking round it. Perhaps they could even hear our voices. But if they were being held against their will why didn't they shout out? And why would Hayter let me near the place?

I wanted to talk it over. But I was not talking to him—very hard. I ignored him severely at the Hall, but since he was ignoring me just as hard, it seemed to cancel out. All of this bubbled and heaved in my head, until I felt like screaming. But I'm not the screaming type. I yell and bellow, but I don't scream.

Talking it through was out. Who with? Yasmin would only shrug and look at me as though I was a suitable case for treatment. Natalie? Forget it. The powers-that-be— certainly not. I'd already had one little exchange with Ms Courtney outside the tithe barn and got out of it at the peril of my immortal soul, as Pa would put it. There was only one possibility, and he was impossible.

If you can't talk about something and thinking about it is driving you up the wall—there's only one thing left. Action.

Come Saturday—yet another fine hot day from the word go—I put on the oldest, least conspicuous clothes I had, and borrowed the binos which Pa had used in his curate days when he was a twitcher. Though how he ever moved quietly through the undergrowth was another mystery beyond my deductive powers.

Taking the long way round, I reached the Haggerton Estate wall near mid-day. I circled it carefully—stopping now and then to check that I was not observed. The school and grounds were all quiet as the grave. My team was playing away, and Prescot was being 'rested' (Ms Frazer still sulking after my let-down over the District Cup).

To my surprise I found Winterbottom's old coat still on the top of the stonework, though I had the distinct feeling it had moved along the wall away from the little gateway. This made me wary as I climbed up.

But once over the wall, clothing intact (jeans this time, not splittable skirt) I dropped into the grass and looked quickly around. No sign of life—human anyway, though the bushes stirred now and then with bird and small animal movements.

I headed for the vantage point of what I now knew was the tomb of wicked Lord Haggerton—No. 13 the guide said.

Coming towards it through waist-high bracken and bushes I saw something which made me laugh at the memory of our ignominious attempt to scale the walls. On the farther side of the tomb, the stonework had collapsed leaving a rough sort of stairway up which one could climb with ease. In half a minute I was on the top and stretched out on the turf that covered it. The autumn sun was warm on my back, the sky blue above, the birds twittered in the trees nearby, and I thought what an agreeable place it would be for a sunbathe—if that's what one wanted.

Unslinging the binos, I flattened a small section of the weeds that fringed the edge of the tomb roof and made myself a kind of sniper lookout. Three metres off the ground gave a truly new view of the world. The red-yellow rear walls of the Hall stood out above the trees. So did the pitched roof of the tithe barn.

Twiddling the knobs of Pa's binos brought the terrace in front of that side of the Hall leaping into view. Two people were sitting at a table there, drinking. One had his back to me but it could only be Cameron Hayter himself. The other must be the gamekeeper. They were deep in some kind of argument. It certainly didn't look like Lord of the Manor giving gamekeeper his orders for the day—

more like business partners talking things over. The question was—what business? Unfortunately the binos didn't run to sound. So I watched.

They finished their drink and began to walk in my direction. Instinctively I ducked down, then remembered they were a good quarter of a mile away. And in any case they were heading for—the tithe barn. I shadowed them there. Their faces seemed alert, even tense, to me—or maybe that was my imagination. But they were talking like equals—not master and servant. It was a funny situation, I thought.

Then they vanished from view round the corner of the tithe barn. From where I lay I couldn't see the doorway. But there was no sign of them appearing on the far side. They must have gone in there. Elementary, my dear Watson. But what for—routine inspection of property or visit to prisoners—if they really were prisoners?

I waited, binos trained on the barn. Nothing moved, except the finger on my watch dial. Five minutes passed. I began to feel bored and slowly began to sweep the area between the Hall and the Old Hag's tomb where I lay, coming back every half minute or so to the tithe barn. No movement.

For the fifth time I traversed the ground, up across the gardens and the terrace and along the frontage of the Hall itself. Then I went stiff and nearly dropped my binoculars.

Someone had stepped onto the balcony—where our party had stood and looked out earlier in the week. It was a girl. In my excitement I sprang upright, fiddled with the controls and her face leapt towards me. She enlarged so suddenly I ducked down as though she were looking straight at me. There was absolutely no doubt—it was

Amelia Hardy. By the time I gathered my wits and looked again the balcony was empty.

I trained on the terrace again and waited. No sign that Hardy was coming out. So back I ranged to the tithe barn and drew blank again. Now I took a wider arc and this time I found the black waters of the mysterious little pool in my lens. It did look haunted. And deep. You could drown in there and no one would see or know, the pike would bare their teeth . . . don't be ridiculous, Prescot!!

Double take. What was that on the bank? Clothing? My imagination was taking me down a time tunnel. My fingers shook as I focused. Not the frilled shirt and breeches of a decadent lord—but jeans and T-shirt. Now I dropped the binos, picked them up and focused again. I knew those clothes—all too well—they belonged to James Winterbottom. The binos shook in my hand but at last my gaze settled on the surface of the pool. It was black and still. I stopped breathing—what had happened?

Not that? In a flash his words to the guide came back to my mind: 'Is it deep enough to drown in?' Biting my lip in a frantic effort to control—what? My thoughts? I scrambled to my feet. Then dropped to my knees again, staring open-mouthed. Like an outsize white frog, James Winterbottom suddenly shot out of the water and into the air, to fall back with a smack. The sound carried across to where I knelt, the binos hanging helplessly in my hands as I began to laugh—partly in relief, but mostly at the sight of the idiot cavorting in the water. Then I remembered—swimming was the only exercise he took— and he was enjoying it.

I realized I might be visible to anyone looking from the Hall and collapsed, still shaking with laughter, onto the grass again. I couldn't help it. I trained the binos on the pool but the spectacle was over. The waters were empty again and the clothes had vanished from the bank along with their owner. Moments passed, but there was no sign of Winterbottom.

Lying still, I listened. Someone was coming my way, pushing through the undergrowth. Aargh, I thought, if he knew I'd been spying on him. Then that notion gave me hysterics again and I pushed my face down into the grass to muffle the sound.

His sounds were not muffled. He was below me now, walking round Old Hag's tomb. I lay as still as I could, heaving and hiccuping now and then. It got worse. He was singing—no, not singing. He was giving an improvisation of a full brass band, one instrument after another, drums thrown in. He was having a ball—and he did not know who was watching and listening.

Perhaps I assumed he wouldn't be able to find his way up and would move on, leaving my little secret intact.

I was wrong, wrong. I heard a noise behind me and half turned. To see Winterbottom as he slowly rose above the edge of the tomb roof.

He reached the level and became aware of my presence in the same second. After an age of paralysis, he spoke.

'You saw me, in the water.'

I sat up swiftly, turning from him, shoulders rigid to control my indecent hilarity and said, with dignity, 'What you do in your spare time has no possible interest for me.'

22 *James*

Now and then during that write-off of a week, I asked myself—did Holmes ever get in a helpless stupid rage, did he ever want the ground to open up and swallow him? Was he ever driven spare with frustration because he needed to talk to someone about his theories and findings and the one person he could talk to he wasn't talking to?

The answer to all these questions was no, of course, he was too bloody cold and logical to get angry or ashamed, much too bloody cold and logical to have a female partner, and he always had Watson to ask him questions at the right time. But the main reason was he was a fictional detective, and I was realizing a bit late in the day that I was a real one with no author around to sort it—in fact, I had to sort it all myself.

One thing kept me going, though. The thought of that pool in the woods. At night when I was in bed I could picture it. Cool under the sun, away from anywhere, away from anyone. By Saturday morning I wasn't thinking about anything else and at eleven o'clock, I was clambering over the estate wall—well away from the gate and the gamekeeper. The undergrowth on the farther side was thick and high and there was only the Evil Earl's tomb sticking up like a small fort to guide me.

I pressed on through bracken and briar, skirting the tomb, though I noted with some relief that on that side there was an easier way up to the top. The going was easier on the way to the pool and, when I reached it, I found the grass on the bank was short. I stopped there for a while, looking and listening. There was no one in sight and only the birds and the bees were making a pleasant sound in the background. It was just right. And right in front of me was a gap in the reeds that fringed the water.

Was this where the thirteenth Lord went in for his last dip? Did he fall or was he pushed? Did the dreaded man-eating pike get him? Pull the other one, I thought as I stripped off.

Oh, mate, it was cold—but only for a second. One foot sank into mud that tickled my toes, the other struck into the deep. Next minute I was in the middle, ducking and thrashing to fight off the first shock. Then it was just right, the water running over my back and sides, smooth as silk.

How deep was it? I kicked my heels up and went down, trawling with my outstretched hands for the bottom. There was none. Down, down I went till the blood began to bang away in my ears. I gave up, jack-knifed, kicked down and drove through black, green, yellow-white water to the top where the sun was shining. Up in the air I shot, and smacked down, making a tremendous racket, till I remembered—James, lad, you are trespassing. If you don't want to be hanged or sent to Australia for life, cool it.

Besides, I was beginning to get cold—cold—cold, under the skin. I did a few more circuits—there wasn't more than twenty metres distance in it—and one or two more plunges, then I made for the shore, dried off with my T-shirt, dressed and headed towards the old tomb. The sun was warm on my back, the birds were singing, no one else was in sight. I was well away from the Hall now, so I marched along giving my well-known impression of the Haggerton Prize Silver Band playing 'Colonel Bogey'. I was up to the bit where the bass drum takes over and the trumpets and trombones begin to counter-march as I clambered up the fallen stones and out onto the warm grassy top of the tomb.

Just for a heart-stopping second my eyes looked straight into Prescot's blue ones under that wild red mop of hair. I realized she'd seen me skinny dipping, but all she said was some remark about my spare time and turned her back on me.

I lay down. The sun was warm on my skin, and she was ignoring me. My eyes half-closed—I kept her red head in view in case she turned round—and I began to relax. Five minutes passed, I was beginning to doze. Suddenly she said:

'We have to talk.'

'Thought you weren't talking.'

'I'm not. Not about your generally dire behaviour; about Adam and Hardy.'

I thought, typical, get one in below the belt, then change the subject. But I remembered Holmes and steeled myself to be cold and logical.

'OK. OK. Let's talk about them,' I began. 'They're in the Hall, at least Adam is.'

'How d'you know?'

'First because I'm sure now that Hayter and Toby are the same and second,' I paused, 'because I found a little chunk of green plastic on top of one of Hayter's computers.'

'So?'

'Not any old chunk of plastic. The tail end of Adam's monster mascot.'

'How d'you know?'

'Got his tooth-marks on.'

'Brilliant!'

'All right, be sarky. But I'm sure now that Hayter's involving Adam in some kind of computer scam—that's what it's all about. Adam would be ideal for that—he doesn't give a toss about the law, the state, etc.'

'What scam?'

'Dunno. I have a gut feeling it has to do with that film script Hayter mentioned—you know, "Eco-Wars".'

'Nothing illegal in a film script—just a story.'

'It may involve people who break the law . . . '

'That's just guesswork!' Prescot was impatient.

'All right, smart-arse. Can you do any better?'

'I can, as it happens. I've just seen Hardy (with my binos). She's at the Hall along with Adam and she didn't look like a prisoner to me.'

I was impressed but didn't show it. I covered up with questions.

'I can see why Adam's working with Hayter (illegal or no) but what's in it for Hardy? Why's she here?'

Prescot was quiet for a moment, then she raised a finger.

'Gottit. Hayter wants a helper. He knows Ma Hardy's boyfriend via the drug net. He pays them to have Hardy lure Adam away. I told you that lottery talk was garbage.'

'Sounds wild to me.'

'All right, smart-arse. Can you do any better?'

As she spoke Prescot burst out laughing. I joined in. It made me feel better.

'OK, OK. So what do we do with our facts and theories?'

She looked serious. 'Let's do it the right way for a start.'

'Right way?'

'Yes. Go and tell Detective Inspector Sharp all we know.'

'That idiot!'

'Whatever you think of him, he's in charge of the case.'

I forced myself to be cool and logical and had to admit, 'OK, OK. We go to Sharp. But I'll do the talking.'

'That'll be fun.'

I remained calm. More minutes ticked by in the warm sunshine. Suddenly her head turned towards me.

'I didn't mean to spy on you swimming, honest!'

23 Emmeline

W hy didn't I object when Winterbottom told me 'I'll do the talking?' Why did I let him take charge? Was it my mother in me again— let the men take the lead? I don't think so. I'm not really like that. Pa says I'm a bully. I just know my natural place is in the front. But if you're supposed to be partners, one can't take the lead all the time. Do you take turns? Who keeps the score?

I've a suspicion, only a suspicion, though, that under all this, the reason (OK, *one* reason) why I didn't object when he took charge is that I wanted to see what would happen—a sort of risk taking, like mental bungee-jumping. I wasn't disappointed. We went straight to the police station in town, Winterbottom lengthening his stride to splitting point to keep in front. Up the worn stone steps we charged, into the corridor which smelt of some vile kind of disinfectant and so up to the battered brown reception desk with a balding, paunchy sergeant sitting behind it.

'Is DI Sharp here?' rapped out Winterbottom, sending the sergeant's whitish eyebrows wiggling to the top of his head.

Back he came with: 'Who wants him and what for?'

Was Winterbottom stopped in his tracks? Not a bit.

'You can say it's about the Crowther–Hardy missing persons case. New—possibly conclusive—evidence.'

The sergeant breathed out, almost began to speak, then with a quick sizing up glance at the two of us, levered himself up and went through a door behind his desk. We waited. Winterbottom did not look at me but I could see the edge of a complacent smile on the corner of his mouth. We waited. Slowly the smile began to droop.

The sergeant came back. Now he had a complacent smile on his lips. He said nothing, just looked at us as though we'd told him a particularly good joke.

'This way, please.'

We turned. Behind us was a small fair-haired WPC. She signalled with her hand and we followed her along the passage, down some dark stairs which seemed to be leading to the toilets—or maybe they had more than once been used as a loo.

Ahead of us an illuminated sign said 'Interview Room'. She pushed open the heavy door and switched on the light, waving us to chairs behind a bare table. Then she sat down demurely in a corner. More waiting till heavy footsteps sounded in the corridor outside. I smiled t the WPC and she gave me a rather stern smile back.

Sharp marched in, switched on a small tape recorder he table, and growled, '14.15 hours Saturday October nterview with Emmeline Prescot and James Winter-' Having thoroughly softened us up he now looked ight—what is the conclusive evidence?'

Winterbottom cleared his throat. 'Adam Crowther and Amelia Hardy are at Haggerton Hall in a false chamber built into the tithe barn. Cameron Hayter is involved in this. His accomplice doubles as gamekeeper and handyman. Motive, possible computer scam, but drugs not ruled out.'

He spread his hands in a sweeping gesture: 'That's about it. A quick raid this afternoon should collar the lot. We'll bow out at this point and you can take all the credit.'

Sharp drummed his fingers on the table; the WPC suddenly decided that blowing her nose meant covering her whole face with her hanky.

'Very generous, Mr Winterbottom. But one question?' Sharp was too polite.

'Yes,' said Winterbottom grandly.

'We get all the credit—that's fine. But, tell me, who will get the blame if all this turns out to be the fantasies of overworked imaginations and Haggerton CID is taken to the cleaners by Hayter's lawyers and the media has a field day at our expense, my promotion prospects go out of the window, and . . . '

To my amazement Winterbottom calmly held up his hand.

'No win, no fee, Inspector. Of course we would take the blame,' Sharp's face suddenly went a shade redder, 'if all this were mistaken. However, we happen to know it's not—not fantasy but facts.'

'My apologies,' murmured Sharp (sarcasm, alas, was wasted), 'but pardon me for asking—what is the evidence?'

Winterbottom smiled and raised his fingers, folding them down one by one.

'My colleague Prescot spotted the false chamber—in a particularly ingenious way by comparing the interior and exterior dimensions of the tithe barn. She has also seen Amelia Hardy on the balcony at Haggerton Hall.'

'Ah,' said Sharp.

'I have personally satisfied myself from a face-to-face encounter that the eyes of the dosser Toby and those of Cameron Hayter are one and the same. What is more,' Winterbottom's voice became triumphal, 'I recovered from Haggerton Hall this conclusive material evidence of the presence there of Adam Crowther. This—I am ninety-eight per cent certain—is the tail from the monster mascot Adam Crowther normally kept on top of his home computer, but missing since his disappearance. A dental records comparison with the tooth-mark clearly visible will be the clincher. Though I have no doubt his next of kin could identify it.'

After a brief pause for effect, Winterbottom finally robbed me of my remaining breath by saying, 'Time is of the essence, Inspector. I have reason to believe that Hayter suspected, during our face-to-face encounter, that I was on to him. He may at this moment be fleeing the country.'

Sharp nodded. 'If he has, it's all a bit late in the day then.' The WPC took refuge behind her hanky again. I felt it was time to intervene.

'He was certainly at the Hall at 12 this morning, nspector—and so was Amelia Hardy.' I rapidly explained hat I had seen from the top of Lord Haggerton's tomb.

'Posing as a bird watcher, no doubt,' he murmured. he reached out, muttered, '14.30 hours', and ed off the tape recorder.

d. I've listened to you with great patience, under

our latest guiding principles of Neighbourhood Watch openness. That I think entitles me to speak with perfect frankness.

'What it amounts to is this: Haggerton CID is to abandon its carefully conducted search for two missing teenagers, and launch a surprise raid, quite illegally, since no magistrate would give us a warrant, on a respected, no, celebrated, member of the community with enormous media attention attached to him,' he underlined the words, 'on suspicion of drug running, computer fraud, abduction—we're talking twenty years inside. And all this on the basis of someone's face seen in a flash of a second from quarter of a mile's distance by a trespasser, the expression in the eyes of a man seen at a range of two feet, guesswork about the measurements of a restored barn, and,' he paused, 'a bit of masticated green plastic.'

The WPC's head was down to her knees. Winterbottom had gone white—with rage, I'm certain—while I had the urge to laugh hysterically. But Sharp hadn't finished yet.

'You two have twice been told, by the school and by me personally—bearing in mind the upset caused to the missing kids' families etc.—to leave this matter alone. You have clearly wilfully ignored those warnings. What the school choose to do is their affair. What I shall do is another matter, if you do not lay off, stay away from Haggerton Hall. Now, WPC Taylor will show you the way out. Good afternoon.'

Sharp marched out. As he reached the door W. called out, 'Can I have that bit of Adam's mascot back if you don't want it?'

'Oh, but I do,' returned Sharp.

'What for?'

'Material evidence for a possible charge of obstructing the course of justice and wasting police time.'

Winterbottom got to his feet to run after Sharp, but I caught him by the arm. Then with WPC Taylor leading the way and me holding tight on to Winterbottom's arm, we proceeded in an orderly fashion back into the street.[8]

---

[8] My feet didn't touch the ground.—J. W.

24 *James*

We stood on the pavement outside the nick for a moment, with WPC Taylor beaming down on us. I was livid. On impulse I turned to march back up the steps again, with the object of disembowelling DI Sharp or some other tension-easing action, but I couldn't move. I was rooted to the spot. Prescot had a grip on my arm, like iron. I glared at her. She must have known it was beneath my dignity to brawl with a female in the street. She spoke soothingly, 'Let's go and have a cup of tea. There's something I want to tell you.'

Curiosity always gets the better of me. I relented and let her lead me to a nearby greasy spoon where she placed me at a table in the far corner, then marched to the counter and ordered two teas as though she were discussing the wine list with the head waiter. I glanced at her tall figure, looming over the cake stand, and wondered, not for the first time in our month-long association, why she always behaved as though she were older than me. Must remember, I thought, to check when her birthday is.

In another stray thought I wondered how I would have managed with a sister—I had no previous experience of spending so much time in female company. Mum, of course, is different as I may have pointed out before.

The tea, dark as bog water, was placed before me and Prescot sat down, leaning forward and speaking low (for her). 'Sorry to drag you out of the nick like that, but I thought it would not be a brilliant idea to be banged up for assaulting a police officer.'

She said this with a broad smile on her freckled face, which made her snub nose twitch—a feature which, observant as I am, I had not paid any attention to before.

She went on, more seriously, 'That apart, what I want to say is not for the ears of WPC Taylor. She was hanging about in a listening mode, you may have noticed.'

I hadn't but didn't say. Instead I asked her, 'What was it that was so urgent and so confidential?'

'Our next step, Holmes, old chap.'

'Which one?' I was still bemused.

'To continue the investigation.'

'I know that, Marple, but how?'

'I'll spell it out. Tonight, when it's dark enough, we shall enter the Haggerton Estate, proceed with discretion to the tithe barn and try to locate the door to the secret chamber . . . '

'You're crazy,' I said. She wasn't listening.

'We shall try and open it. If we fail, as no doubt we shall, we shall talk to the prisoners—if they are there, of course.'

I decided to humour her in this manic scheme. 'How?'

'Somewhere, since that chamber has no windows, there must be a ventilator.'

'Good thinking, Marple.' If she heard the sarcasm she ignored it.

A shadow of a frown crossed her face but she went on. 'If they are inside, we shall discreetly phone the police.'

'How—call at the Hall and ask to use theirs?'

'No, I shall borrow Pa's mobile phone.'

'Will he lend it?'

'If his daughter tells him she will be staying overnight with friends he will gladly do so, because, despite his generally irritating manner, he tends towards the protective. I suggest you give your mum the same story.'

She was involving me against my will. 'Suppose there's no sign of them in the tithe barn?' I asked.

'Then we try and find a way into the Hall. If we really believe they are held there, then we should not give up until we've found them. And since the forces of law and order are doing nothing, we have to. If they are there of their own free will, then at least we can find out why.'

'All this,' I remarked, with fine irony, 'doesn't sound very much like Miss Marple, does it?'

She gave me a keen look.

'Stuff Miss Marple and stuff Sherlock Holmes. This is Prescot and Winterbottom, who have their own methods.'

'You mean Winterbottom and Prescot, don't you?'

'My way trips off the tongue better.'

'That's your story.'

'OK, OK, you say it your way, I'll say it mine.'

She thrust a hand across the table. We shook, rose in silence, and left the caff.

At eleven that evening we sat on the grass at the top of the Clough waiting for dark to fall. We were both dressed in black or as near as we could manage, with our gear (for parental benefit) in rucksacks. I'd brought a thickish walking stick which Mum had for her fell walking. Prescot touched it.

'Hey, what's this for?'

'This is for if the opposition turns up.'

'Couldn't you find your service revolver?'

'Give over, Prescot. Come on. It's dark enough.'

Over the wall, amid the trees and bushes and the waist-high bracken, it seemed darker still. We made our way slowly, since we had to, and as quietly as possible. Every now and then, a breaking stick or a whippy branch made a noise that stopped us in our tracks. But all was quiet except for those strange small sounds you get in the country at night with wicked little hunters going after shivering little game.

The tithe barn showed up suddenly against the darkening sky. We halted again, then began to move round the walls. I found one door by touch. It was locked. Prescot touched me on the shoulder. 'That's the main door. I think we want a door on the Hall side at the other end.'

The undergrowth had given way to shorter grass. We were getting to the garden area. Round the next corner we shrank back as we saw upstairs windows still lit—the light spilling out on to the lawn.

'They can't see us from there,' I urged and we moved on keeping close to the barn wall with its rough timbers.

'Ah!' Prescot, who was now in front, turned. 'Here's a door.'

I joined her. The door was small and smooth, quite

unlike the main door with its studded oak. This one was new.

'This must be it.'

'Yeah, and it's locked. Let's feel round for the ventilator. You do that side. I'll do this.'

We searched the wall on either side of the door, inch by inch, but found nothing. Then Prescot, on tiptoe, found it.

'Here—it's about three metres up.'

She turned, bumping into me. 'Look, you get on to my shoulders and I'll hoist you up. Come on—you're lighter than me.'

'OK,' I muttered reluctantly, and began to clamber up on her bent back. But I never made it. Something spun me round. I rolled on the grass, scrambled up. Two of them, dark-clad like us, had come out of the dark, silent and quick. I had the smaller one. The bigger one had grabbed Prescot and seemed to be snatching at her clothes.

Forgetting Number Two in my sudden fury, I lunged at the big one and fetched him a terrific clout with Mum's walking stick. He swore, let Prescot go, then grabbed her again. But just as I swung up the stick to let him have a second blow, Number Two, I think, hit me behind the ear such a belt that it threw me down against the wall.

I was just aware of three things—the door opening, me being dragged over the threshold, and Prescot whispering:

'Opposition, one; Home Team, nil.'

Then all the dark round me rushed into my head and I passed out.

25 Emmeline

I pushed myself up from where I'd been thrown and hurled myself against the door which was swiftly closing. But our attackers were too strong. It swung to with a quiet, well oiled click. The unknown space around me was pitch black and silent save for the background hum of an air-conditioner.

They hadn't taken my torch and it still worked. I swung the beam to the ground. W. lay there, still and quiet, face white. I must have more light. The torch beam swung over the rough plastered outer wall of the barn, then back to blank whiteness—false ceiling maybe a foot above my head, false wall a few feet to my left. No switches. Were they outside? This *was* a prison.

I crouched down at W.'s side, listened to his heart. That seemed OK. His breathing was regular. I made a pillow out of my rucksack and jacket.

The torch again, and I saw, perhaps two metres in front of me, a door. Locked? I reached it in two steps and it opened easily. Beyond in the torch beam I saw a kind of bed-sit cell, the sort you get in prisons where they invite TV cameras. A bed in the corner, half covered with a rumpled duvet, an easy chair, a table, and ah! a bedside lamp. I switched it on. There were no light switches on the wall here either.

Now back to Winterbottom. I dragged him along the passage, across the floor and then heaved him on to the bed. He was heavier than I'd imagined. I sat beside him and listened again to his breathing wishing I'd paid more attention in Girl Guide First Aid classes.

He was conscious. I was suddenly aware as I bent over him that he was studying me with analytical interest. Our eyes met, he looked away and I was suddenly relieved, thinking to myself—if he can be embarrassed he can't be concussed—though First Aid classes never mentioned this kind of test. Winterbottom was clearly wide awake, now.

'How long have I been here?'

'Don't you mean—where am I?'

'Stop messing about. I know where I am.'

'Well, you've been out for about five minutes.'

He felt his head carefully with his fingers.

'Don't touch,' I told him. 'You've got a lump like a hairy duck's egg behind your ear, but there's no bleeding.'

'Yeah, that little bloke, Hayter's No. 2, must have coshed me.'

'That's a point. Why didn't you hit him rather than going for the big one?'

He looked down for a second then said, 'He was trying to strip you.'

I giggled. 'He was after my mobile phone, not my virtue.'

'And he got it—the phone?'

I nodded. 'Afraid Plan A is off. We're stuck here unless we can find a way out.'

'Look,' he said, 'let's get a bit of rest. We can't do anything right now.' He eyed me. 'Where are you going to lie down?'

'On the bed, if you can move over a bit.'

He obliged. There was just room. I let him have the pillow. Leaning over I switched off the bed lamp and for a few moments we lay in silence. Then he spoke.

'I suppose we are the only ones here? You know— Adam and Hardy must be with Hayter and the other bloke.'

'Do you think they'll hang about now after this?'

'Dunno. Look, let's try and sleep, eh?'

But sleep was a long way off. The next moment, on went an overhead light. We both sat up, blinking and staring.

The dark wall had partly slid back and in the opening, dressed in creased pyjamas, his eyes bleary, was Adam Crowther.

'If you must doss in here, then you might do it quietly —Oh! It's you two! Might have known. Investigating, I suppose, and now you're banged up like me.'

'Are you alone here?' I asked.

'I was.'

I ignored the sarcasm. 'Where's Hardy?'

His face suddenly looked miserable. 'Gone off with Hayter by now, I should think.'

'That figures,' said Winterbottom sympathetically.

'No, it doesn't.' Adam's face was suddenly angry. 'You don't understand. Nobody does.'

Winterbottom sat up shaking his head and wincing at

the same time: 'If we don't understand then you've got some explaining to do, Adam. You're a prisoner now, but a few days ago you weren't. You were in Hayter's computer room leaving bits of your mascot around.'

'Yes,' I put in, 'and Hardy was out on the balcony this afternoon. So what's going on, Adam?'

For a few seconds he stared at us in silence, then slowly sat down in the easy chair.

'OK. I'll tell you—but only as long as you pass nothing on to anybody else, right—not police, not school.'

Winterbottom looked doubtful but I said, 'Go on, Adam. Let's have it—what's your story?'

26 *Adam*

I know what you think—what everybody thinks—
Amelia's behind this. She lured me here.

You've got it wrong: that big-mouthing, drugging,
it's all a front. She's naïve, easily led, and—she's as
miserable as hell. As to who got the pair of us into this
mess—it was me.

I can see what you're thinking—pull the other. The
truth about Amelia is this. Three years ago her dad left
home. She worshipped him and it knocked her off the
rails. Then her mother's new bloke moved in and started
playing the heavy father—straightening Amelia out. She
made up her mind to clear out and try to find her real
dad.

Now this shows how innocent she is. She thought she
could get money together by pushing at school. It wasn't
really her idea. It was Scully's, the scumbag. He used her
as a front. If there was any comeback, it'd be her operation
not his.

Amelia was in it up to her neck when we first got in touch, via the Net, quite by chance. She worked out who I was very quickly. She told me everything. She knew she could trust me. I listened and didn't rubbish what she said.

We started to try and work out how she could leave home. I got so involved, I was going to sell my computer to help her. But I wanted her out of the drug pushing. You can stare. The thing is she needed help and no one was helping but me.

Then out of the blue, this hacker (code name Maizie— I know, hackers are a bit funny) contacted me. It was frightening at first because he knew I was the one who'd hacked into the supermarket computer and priced everything down. Don't ask me how he knew. Hayter knows everything he needs to know.

He wasn't about to shop me. He thought I was just the person he wanted for a big secret operation to bring together all the eco-action groups in a grand slam to finish off GM crop trials altogether. He had good cover, he reckoned he was big in show business, and was working on this film called *Eco War*.

Would I join him? He'd pay well. Stuff the money, I told him. It's a good cause. I was at a loose end in cyberspace. Then I had an inspiration. In return you can help my friend get away from home. At first he was iffy about it, then suddenly he changed his mind. We were picked up by this bloke called Venables and taken to Haggerton Hall. Venables fixed up the Newcastle letters. We were half a mile away from the school when everyone thought we were up north—except you two.

At first it was a dream. I was happy. You've seen Hayter's computer room. And when Amelia found out that 'Maizie' really was heart-throb Cameron Hayter, she was over the moon. When he promised her that after the operation was over he'd find her father for her, she was ecstatic. She didn't need me any more—or at least she thought she didn't.

No one had to know we were there. As soon as a warning bell sounded we went into this apartment in the tithe barn and stayed there till the all-clear came. I remember the day the school party came round. It was risky, of course it was, but Hayter lived on risk. One day he was attending one of these government cultural jamborees, the next he was working on his scam to finish off GM research for good.

Venables was tough but even he thought Hayter played a dangerous game. But double bluff was meat and drink to Hayter. He'd played it before, juggling millions in bank accounts. And now he had a bolt hole, a tax haven island called Santa Rosa in the Caribbean. If everything went pear-shaped, he'd head there. Haggerton Hall was a pile of bricks to him.

I didn't care what he got up to. I like his Eco Wars scam. He'd agreed to do what I couldn't—help Amelia. That's what counted for me. He was crafty. He knew he could count on me as long as he helped Amelia. What the law thought about Hayter didn't bother me.

Until I realized one day that Eco Wars was a triple cross. It put him in touch with all the secret environmental action groups. Then, on the quiet, he was shopping them, not to the police but to the security teams in the big business bio-tech companies. They went in for dirty tricks and they paid him well. I understood that Hayter loved excitement but most of all he loved money, endless amounts of it.

I felt dirty. But what could I do, my private plans were locked in to his. Still, two can play the double game. Computers are made for that. I began, secretly, to tip off the eco action groups. I think I sabotaged quite a bit of his operation.

Hayter began to suspect what I was up to. He was always on the alert. I overheard him tell Venables that 'a kid with a face like a ferret', (sorry, Jim) had sussed out that 'Toby' was a disguise. When he found the same kid (in the school party) snooping around the computer room, Hayter was sure he'd removed something but didn't know what. Then I guessed my ploy of leaving a chunk of the monster mascot around had worked. You knew I was in the Hall. After that Hayter began to check up on my computer work.

Then Amelia spotted Emmeline standing on the top of the old tomb and Hayter knew it was time to move.

I was locked up because I knew too much about his operation. Amelia was free but she was no problem. She'd stick with him. They were to go together with her posing as Vivienne Thorley, a stepdaughter. By this time, she would follow Hayter anywhere. Venables, who prefers Old England to Santa Rosa, would go his own way, but after forty-eight hours he'd give the police an anonymous tip-off about the lodger in the tithe barn. There was only supposed to be one of us until you two barged in.

Late in the day I realized that Hayter would dump Amelia en route. Once they were away she was no more use to him. And on Santa Rosa they're quite happy about money laundering, but Interpol and abduction of minors is another matter.

So, before I was put in here I managed to send a

coded message to security at Manchester Airport telling them that Vivienne Thorley was missing person Amelia Hardy.

And that's about it.

27 *James*

Listening to Adam's story took me right back to our chat—ages back—when I asked him to be my partner in the detection business.

'That's what comes of being an idealist, isn't it?' I jeered. 'Some crook makes a monkey of you—and in the end you have to work with the law, don't you?'

He flared back at me: 'Look at you two. You work with the law and where does it get you? Banged up with a stupid idealist.'

'Children, children,' said Prescot, raising a hand as though she was her father blessing the congregation. 'It's nearly midnight. No time for squabbles. Let's get things sorted. Numero uno. How long are we banged up for?'

'Hayter told me,' said Adam quietly, 'that when they left, the generator and the lock to this place would be on a forty-eight-hour time switch. If no one else comes, we walk out after two days. And, as insurance, on the third day Venables is to give the law an anonymous tip-off.'

Prescot smiled, 'All very fine. If Hayter told the truth.'

'Oh, I don't think he'd lie—don't laugh—about something like that. He's a con man not a homicidal maniac.'

'Fair enough. But I think we can do a bit better than that. By Sunday lunch my parents or Winterbottom's mum will start to ask questions.'

'So,' I put in, 'we've got anything from twelve hours upwards in this hole. What about food or water?'

Adam looked doubtful. 'Two days' supply of both—for one.'

Prescot nodded. 'Right, well, I'll take charge of that in case one of you two tries to push the other one out of the lifeboat.'

'Very funny,' I muttered. 'Anyway, I'm off food for now.'

'There's only one snag,' Adam said, eyeing us both. 'Once the generator broke down—while we were in here. That wasn't funny.'

'How?'

'Pitch black for one thing—not dark—just nothing, couldn't even see what time it was. And the air began to get—well—think, the portaloo stink takes over.'

'That's bearable,' began Prescot.

'It was—it only lasted half an hour—then.'

All three of us said nothing while we thought that one through.

Prescot broke the silence. 'Well, I think it's time for beddy-byes. Let's put the lights out and go to sleep.'

Adam nodded, got up and went to his own cell. 'I'll leave the door open. The thingy's in a cubbyhole between your bit and mine. Try and use it quietly if you have to.' He paused as if embarrassed, then 'Goodnight,' he murmured and disappeared.

Prescot rolled on to the bed beside me.

'You have the duvet, OK?'

'Don't need it. I feel too warm anyway.'

'All the same.'

There was a faint click from next door, then it was dark. Dark for real, just like Adam said. Like being in a box. I began to feel uneasy. Maybe Prescot felt the same for she suddenly giggled. 'If Ma could see her daughter now she'd have kittens.'

I started to laugh but stopped. It sent pain-waves through my skull. I gritted my teeth.

'Goodnight.'

'Goodnight.'

I must have passed out. I was in a nightmare. I was in a wood, a jungle, twisting and turning as creepers and thorns clutched and scratched.

'What's up?' Prescot's hand was on my shoulder.

'Nightmare. What time is it?'

'Can't see and I'm not switching that lamp on just for that. Come on now.'

I blacked out again. I was in a dark tunnel. I reached out in a panic and must have knocked Prescot.

'Oh, my nose, you clown.'

'Sorry. Never been in the same bed with anyone in my life before.'

'Me neither. It takes practice.'

We lay in silence for a while, facing one another. I could feel her breath on my face. She whispered, 'Tell you something.'

'Like what?'

'I'm sorry I said what I said on the Clough, about your dad.'

'Forget it. Anyway, I bought it—talking about your

great-gran's diary. I hadn't meant to tell you but I got carried away.'

'Well, we're even Stephens now. Funny how it blew up, that row, out of nothing.'

'I think it all came out of something your mother said to me.'

She put her hand on my mouth.

'Tell you what. If you don't tell me what my mum said, I won't tell you what yours said.'

'That's an offer I can't refuse. It's a mug's game.'

'What is?'

'Detection.'

'Yeah, look where it's landed us.'

'No, I don't mean that. I meant we shouldn't have been so eager to investigate each other. You can know too much about someone.'

'OK. But what we know goes no further.'

'It's a deal.'

'How's the head?'

'Buzzing. Let's try and sleep.'

Down into the pit again. My lungs felt as though they were burning—I gasped and gulped. But every time I breathed in I choked again on a thick stench. Reaching out I snapped on the bedside lamp. It didn't work.

'What's going on?' Prescot pulled at me.

'I think it's happened—the generator.'

'You're right. This place is beginning to smell like a sewer.'

'It feels like a furnace. You know, unless we get some fresh air in through the slot in the ventilator, we'll be in trouble.'

'Right. How long d'you reckon the oxygen will last

with three of us converting it to CO_2—and the portaloo adding a quota of methane etc.?'

'You've got a funny sense of humour. Anyway, I'm no good at maths. All we can do is lie still, not use up too much energy.'

'Stop breathing—like hibernating animals.'

'Do they?'

'Do they what?'

'Hibernating animals stop breathing?'

'Don't think so, actually. Just slow down the metabolic rate, don't they?'

'How?'

'No idea. Never been one of the lower animals. Let's stop talking and sleep.'

Gradually, in the foul silence, we dozed off, woke, slept again, in suffocating nightmares. Then I was awake, head on fire and hot slime surging up my throat.

'What is it?' Prescot was awake, her hand on my head; but all I could say was, 'Sick.'

She sprang off the bed and helped me on to the floor and we went in a crouching crawl together, she guiding me into the grisly cubicle where the chemical closet stood. She held my head while I threw up, throat raw, then wiped my face and led me blindly to the bed and we lay down.

But not for long. My head began to spin. I struggled up and back we went to that fetid hole and again till I was drained, and fell back weakly on to the bed.

Now I was delirious and my body shook. I was flaming hot and freezing cold by turns. Prescot pulled the duvet over me, dragged it back when I threw it off, holding it fast with her arm until I fell unconscious for sheer exhaustion. Our night in this dark hole went on and on—there was no break in it, no end.

Until we came to, both of us, with a great leap that almost threw us off the bed. From somewhere came an enormous dull, booming thud. And another and another, like a bombardment. The walls and the ceiling shook, plaster showered down on us.

With a terrific crash the outer door fell in. A blast of delicious fresh air flung the cell door open and swept over us.

From beyond the glare of daylight someone shouted, 'Police. Anyone in there?'

Prescot shouted back, 'Three, one ill.'

'Blimey,' answered the voice. 'There's only supposed to be two.'

28 Emmeline

While the ambulance carried Winterbottom to hospital the police car carried Adam back to the bosom of his family—and then perhaps to the bosom of DI Sharp—while I returned to mine in time for the Sunday roast.

I grovelled to mother, because it was she who rescued us. Early on Sunday morning while Pa was at communion she had this unquenchable urge to talk to her daughter (check up on her). No answer from the mobile naturally, so she began to ring all those who might be harbouring me. Later in the morning she reached Winterbottom's mum who sensibly suggested not 999 but a call to the local nick.

Here by a stroke of luck an alert duty sergeant thought that a second pair of Haggerton Highers missing sounded like carelessness and rang DI Sharp at home where he had just put his bachelor's fish fingers on the hotplate. He switched off the gas and called out the heavy squad, knowing exactly where to send them—being a bit of a Sherlock Holmes himself.

They kept Winterbottom in hospital for a day or two with suspected concussion and I did my Lady Bountiful bit with chocs. He was not very entertaining, spending most of his time sleeping. But on the third day he was wide awake, fully dressed and sitting in an armchair reading a battered copy of *The Valley of Fear*. As we chatted, who should enter (with more chocs) but DI Sharp and Ms Courtney, no less? They sat down and we all four enjoyed an embarrassed silence.

DI Sharp spoke first. 'I owe you an apology—I think. A lot of what you discovered—and quite correctly informed me about—was relevant.'

A self-satisfied smile spread over Winterbottom's face. I simpered demurely.

'That dosser *was* Hayter. The two kids *were* at the Hall all the time. The plastic bit, as it turned out, did have Adam's fingerprints on it, though by the time I got the report, I already had the lad himself . . . '

'Then why didn't you . . . ?' began Winterbottom, but DI Sharp held up his hand.

'We had our own—coincidental—investigation. Our IT people had a notion something dodgy was going on, a string of activities which had a connection—if only we could figure it: computer bank fraud never tracked down, the supermarket price hacker . . . '

At this point Winterbottom and I exchanged glances, but our lips were sealed. DI Sharp, if he noticed this, ignored it.

' . . . and finally, this eco-warrior network. When we got wind of the *Eco War* film, our IT people began, discreetly, to look at Hayter, and his friend Venables, who

is . . . known to us. All right, Jim lad, I'm coming to it.
At first I was irritated with you—and you, too, Ms
Prescot,' said he giving me a glance which boosted my
ego no end. 'I did not see any link between Amelia Hardy
and Adam Crowther, at first, and then certainly not a link
between them and Hayter. But then we learned more
about Adam. (Yes, I know he was the Supermarket
Hacker—he told me afterwards when I guaranteed no
prosecution.) So when the connection became clear,
what we needed to know was—were Adam and Amelia
at Haggerton Hall?'

'Just what we were investigating, Inspector,' broke in
Winterbottom, his nose twitching keenly.

'Ah, but we were concerned that (a) you might put
yourselves in danger and (b) you might trigger off a
change in Hayter's plans before we were ready . . . '

At this point Ms Courtney began to blush—something
so remarkable I treasure the sight still. DI Sharp went on.
'I had confidential consultations with Ms Courtney and
we worked out an entirely unofficial line of enquiry.'

'Ooh!' I burst out. DI Sharp pressed on.

'She made two visits to the Hall. She enquired casually
about the tithe barn and got a very suave put-off from
Hayter about concealing unsightly metal supports to the
end wall. He always had an answer.'

'He's an actor after all,' I said.

'He played several parts at once,' answered DI Sharp
warmly. 'But after the school visit we guessed that if
Adam and Amelia were at the Hall, they were volunteers
not conscripts—why else didn't they try to shout out?'

'Our point entirely,' remarked Winterbottom complacently.

'So more suspicions, but no proof,' went on DI Sharp

imperturbably. 'What made life difficult was I began to suspect someone in our midst was passing the word to Hayter. That was why I rubbished your evidence, when you came to the station on Saturday last.'

'Aha, WPC Taylor,' I cried. 'I misconstrued her simper.'

'Right,' DI Sharp nodded. 'A besotted Hayter fan, who didn't see anything wrong in what he was doing.'

Winterbottom placed his hands together. 'Actually, Hayter wasn't doing anything illegal—just despicable— informing on the eco warriors to the biochem people.' He paused then asked, 'So why should he take off to Santa Rosa?'

Sharp laughed grimly. 'Hayter might not be worried by the law but he knew that once the eco warriors knew what his game was some of them might take their revenge. The biter bit.'

'So he's safe on Santa Rosa,' I said.

'Not necessarily,' returned DI Sharp. 'We've had our sights on his earlier dealings. We were trying to track him and link his computer activities to a series of high-level bank frauds in the City, but he was always one step ahead of us. Whether we could get him extradited for false imprisonment . . .'

'Couldn't you collar Venables?' I asked.

'If we could lay hands on him, we would. But that's a matter of time.'

'What about Hardy?' I demanded at last. 'I take it she didn't fly to Santa Rosa?'

He shook his head. 'Just as I was calling out the heavy squad, security at Manchester Airport told me they had found Amelia Hardy wandering around. Hayter had seen them coming, dumped her, driven to a private airport, taken a two-seater over to Holland and resumed his stately progress to Santa Rosa.'

'Poor old Hardy,' I murmured. 'The last thing she wanted was to come home.'

'There's a happy ending,' put in Ms Courtney. 'Amelia's mother gave the would-be stepfather his marching orders. She's lost a boyfriend and got back her daughter.'

'Meanwhile Hayter gets away with it?' said Winterbottom disgustedly.

'Well, no doubt he's looking over the small print on his eco-war film contract. Whether or not the TV companies will go ahead with it, when every activist group in the country will be out for blood, remains to be seen. I reckon someone, somewhere, will catch up with him, if we don't first.'

DI Sharp got up to go at last. So did Ms Courtney which caused Winterbottom and me to exchange merry glances. As she turned to go Ms Courtney said to us, 'Half term starts this weekend. I don't really expect to see James at school in the meanwhile. I suppose it is no use advising you strongly against pursuing your careers in crime. Next time you may not be so lucky.'

Lucky? Winterbottom and I exchanged glances again but said nothing. Ms Courtney and DI Sharp left together.

Winterbottom looked at me in a funny way. 'I'm going home tomorrow. They've signed me off—bump's gone down. Want to feel?'

He inclined his head but I declined the offer.

'What you doing on Saturday?' he asked.

'Not a lot, at the moment.'

'Tell you what. I'm going to the Haggerton pool for a

swim. Weather's bound to be hot again. Then I'll, like, sunbathe on top of the tomb.'

He paused. 'Want to join me?'

I shrugged. 'I might.'

James
and
29 Emmeline

'Aargh! that was freezing.'
    'What was?'
    'The water, you idiot.'
'Never. Cool and smooth.'
'Then why have you turned blue with goosebumps?'
'I've got a rare blood group.'
'Is there anything else I ought to know?'
'You've found out enough already.'
'Who's talking? Hey! The sun's lovely and warm up here on top of Old Hag.'
'Yeah. I could stay up here all holiday.'
'No such luck. New people here on Monday. Tight security.'
'What sort of people?'
'Lottery winners.'
'Oh no. They'll cut down the woods and plant Leylandii.'
'You know what. You're an elitist!'

'Takes one to know one.'

'Pity all this caper's over. I enjoyed it.'

'Yeah, being buried alive's a giggle.'

'You know you'd do it again.'

'True. Maybe we could set up in business—like Winterbottom and Prescot.'

'You mean Prescot and Winterbottom.'

'No I don't—anyway, what's in a name?'

'Do you mind yours?'

'I mind stupid jokes about it.'

'Did they call you Snowbum in Juniors?'

'Shut up.'

'And Frozen-arse at the High?'

'You say that again, I'll strangle you.'

'That'll put paid to the partnership.'

'Yeah, but it'll be a ready-made mystery.'

'Which you wouldn't dare solve.'

'I could disguise it as suicide.'

'That bump on the head did affect you after all.'

'OK, OK. Tell ya what. D'you think we'll still have intellectual affinity when we're old and grey?'

'I shan't go grey. I'll go rust-coloured.'

'My dad went bald.'

'There's no answer to that. Mm, it's great up here in the sun.'

'You'll make me sneeze—doing that.'

'Funny way you're wired up.'

'None of us are perfect.'

'No, but you grow on me—Snowbum.'

'If I thought you'd said that I'd strangle you.'

'That's a funny way of going about it . . .'

'I got distracted . . .'